KING OF SHADOWS

AMELIA WILDE

For my husband, who sings with me anyway,

even when we know how it ends.

1

PERSEPHONE

SHE WON'T LET me go.

My mother digs her fingers into the flesh of my upper arm, her grip so hard I'm certain it's gone down to the bone. A dishcloth dangles from her other hand. She wouldn't dare crush the dishcloth like this—not something embroidered with a blood-orange poppy. I stitched it when I was six years old. The fact that I made it gives it none of its value. The flower is everything. Flowers are always everything.

"The city? Again?" The quiet words are a perfect match for the buttery sunlight coming in through the double panes over the sink and splashing against the heavy wooden table that takes up most of the kitchen. Early summer, and everything outside blooms lush and green. From here, I can't see the fence that surrounds the house and my mother's fields. I can't see much of anything, with her standing so close. "I already told you it's too dangerous. Besides, you have the spring planting to do."

I plant my feet on the floor and try to visualize being a tree. This is the yoga move I'm shittiest at in general. I'd rather be moving, but if I move at all, she'll only hold tighter. Pain throbs through my arm. I want her to let go, but I want her lightning-bolt attention too. I want her to love me enough to let me go.

She'll leave marks if this goes on much longer.

Then why do other girls get to live in the city? I want to ask. She let me go to school for three years. I only saw the city once. Once, and I paid for it dearly. One time, I went with two friends to an antique bookstore in a snug alley that sells first editions and rare prints, owned by three women whose long dresses reminded me of uniforms, only they had subtle differences. An asymmetrical hem. A bright red scarf. A gold headband twining into chestnut hair. *You're hurting me*, I want to say. What comes out instead is: "You don't need me to do the spring planting. There are employees for that."

Her grip tightens, a bruising cymbal crash of pain, and then she releases me. Steps back. Takes a long breath in. A pang of disappointment vibrates through the center of me like a strike on a tuning fork. Why am I possibly disappointed by the release? Probably because nobody looks at me the way my mother looks at me. With...intensity.

Not until recently, anyway.

A match strikes, hidden beneath flesh and bone, but I don't let her see the warm glow of hope. She's not the only one anymore. His existence is what gave me the courage to bring up the possibility of leaving one last time. "You think my precious flowers should be planted by *employees?*"

My hand goes to my arm in spite of myself and I rub at the tender heat, crane my neck to see if she left a mark. Red fingerprints, that's all I can see. It's anyone's guess whether they'll darken into shadowy bruises or fade away in the sunlight. "No, of course not." I cover them with my hand. "It was only an idea I had, the city. You're right. It's too dangerous."

She whips the dishcloth onto a hook below the sink, the set of her jaw apocalyptic. Once, she let slip that men in the city knew her for her beauty, and I believe it. If she went there now, they'd still talk about her. Her hair, even at forty, is gloriously bronze, curls springy and full. She gathers that hair at the nape of her neck and glares out the window while she pushes it into an elastic. My heart flutters beneath the skin of my neck. She could be a figure in a painting, standing tall and proud at the window, the sun kissing her face.

But a painting would only capture the fine burgundy of her outfit and the way her tunic pinches in at the waist, and her pants fall in a graceful line over shapely legs. She has the tunics specially made to match her image as an earth-mother, a lady of the dirt and plants. The opposite of all the businesswomen in the city, with their pantsuits and silk shells. I would kill for a silk shell, honestly. I'm tired of linen, linen, linen, linen for miles. My mother's legs, in linen like everything else she wears, are a direct result of all the work she does, also part of her image. There are some farms where people hire out all the work, but she gets her hands dirty. I've seen the brochures she keeps in the tiny room she calls an office—thick white paper, a photo of her on the front. In the photo she's grinning in a wash of golden-hour sunset and literally holding a handful of dirt. That could be me. So, so easily. Wouldn't she love that, if I stepped up and took her place?

A painting of my mother in this moment would never capture that latent electricity in the air. A storm coming in. All the softness of the kitchen—the cheery checked tablecloth, the matching curtain at the window—is an illusion. There is nothing soft here.

Her thunder-dark gaze snaps to mine and I almost—almost—take a step backward. "I didn't raise you to be a sheep, Sepphie." The sharpness of her voice is as loving as I've ever heard it. "What does the city have for you? Glass and concrete. Dangerous men who'll rape you as soon as they'll look at you."

"No, they—"

"The city has violence." She sweeps across the kitchen, and this time I do turn—I can't help myself. This time her hand on my arm is a featherlight touch. She skims me across the kitchen floor and opens the door with a graceful tug. My mother takes us several paces out into the yard, my bare feet sinking into the loamy dirt and the flawless carpet of grass, and arrests my momentum with a yank on my shoulder. "What do you see, Sepphie?" Her breath on my ear is hot, her hand soft on my shoulder but no less terrifying.

"The mountain."

Despite everything—despite my dry lips and parched throat and the slow anxious turn of my stomach—irritation sparks like a stubborn ember at the pit of my gut. "The mountain," she repeats. "And who lives in the mountain?"

I can see the gash of his fortress even from here, though it's miles away. Only a very rich man would carve a mansion into the side of a mountain, and the man who lives there is very, very rich. I've heard other rumors, too—that the inside of the mountain is a diamond mine, that the inside of the mountain is worse than a diamond mine, that the diamond mine is a front for terrible things. There's no need to stand here and look at it. The mountain can't come to us. "Luther Hades."

The sooner we can get this two-person play over with, the sooner I can get out into the field. My mother was right about one thing—it was a mistake to say anything to her about moving out of the house. Even though I'm twenty. Even though it's time. She turns me to face her, one swift movement. Her gray eyes, silvery in the golden hour, bore into mine. "And what happens to pretty girls who go into the city unprotected? What would happen to you?"

I didn't say I would go unprotected, I want to shout at her. But that would give everything away, wouldn't it? It would. The words come out well-rehearsed. "He would find me, and he would kill me."

"That's right." She screws up her lips, and for a flash of a second all her bravado drops away. It's back again in the next breath. "He would kill you." My mother raises a hand to my face and draws her fingers down the side of my cheek. "And I can't let that happen. Don't you understand that?"

"But why?" She's said this so many times, and today, *today,* I can't stand not knowing why. I believe her. She's said it so many times that it's hard *not* to believe her. Even if there's no reason. "Why are you so sure he's going to kill me?"

"Does it matter why?"

"I'm twenty years old now, mama. I deserve to know the truth."

"You're still a child. Far too innocent for the city. Too innocent to face the likes of Luther Hades." She stares out at the mountain, narrow-eyed, almost as if she's challenging him to come down to her field right now and try to get to me.

"He's never even met me. Why would he want to kill me?"

"Because that's what men like him do, all of them, every one. The city crawls with them. You'd never get out in one piece." She brushes a lock of hair away from her cheek. "Trust me."

And we're back at the beginning again. He will kill me because men are killers. Because men are rapists. Because men are *dangerous.* Especially men with money.

I understand a lot of things, but this obsession she has with Luther Hades, this burning hatred shining in her eyes—I don't understand that. If all men are ruthless killers, then why does she hire them to work for her? There are other questions—questions I don't dare ask. Like what happened when she met

Luther Hades. She must have met him. You can't hate a person you've never met. Not like this.

Can you?

Her eyes on mine tug at a far corner of my memory. The day I stitched my first poppy into the dishcloth, following a pattern she'd ordered from a catalogue. Her face, pale. *Get into the closet and don't make a sound.* I shake it out of my head. Who can count on memories from fourteen years ago? And why, honestly why, would a man I've never met kill me? A secret reason? Something I've done, without knowing I've done it? Impossible. I haven't done anything. She's never allowed me to do anything. A soft ache pulses at the center of my heart. For so long, I believed that my mother knew everything. Now I think she's a sad, paranoid woman who just wants to keep me here so she won't be lonely, and it's easier to keep me here if I have nowhere else to go.

I let my shoulders sag a little. "I trust you. I won't ask again."

My mother catches my hand in hers and squeezes. The fingerprints on my arm smart. She takes a deep breath. "Are you working in the south fields today?"

I put on a smile. "No, I finished those yesterday."

"There's my good girl."

Does she buy it? I wonder if she does while I collect the specially made basket I take into the fields, the one with ridges at the bottom to keep the blooms separate from one another. While I wave at her through the dining room window. While she paces with her phone pressed to her ear—the phone she keeps locked in her bedside table at night.

In a way, I told the truth. I do understand why she wants to keep me behind her fifteen-foot fences and away from the world. I've read enough books to know that mothers have some base instinct to protect their children, even if that instinct is only biological. In my mother's case, it can't be emotional. Like a less-valuable flower, I am one of the creations she can control.

I told the truth.

But in so many other ways, I lied.

2

PERSEPHONE

Decker meets me at a gap in the fence a full two hours later. A gap—it's not a gap, not empty space per se. At this stretch of the fence the metal slats give way to a chain-link gate. The sight of him hopping to his feet sets off a fluttering feeling low in my belly. "Persephone." The late-afternoon sun glows brighter in his eyes, which are green as the leaves and shot through with yellow the color of the tulips in my mother's greenhouse. He twines his fingers through the metal. "I almost gave up on you." That grin. That joke. He would never.

I drop the basket into the grass at the base of the fence and curl my fingers over his. He looks good in his jeans and white t-shirt. Modern, if not entirely fresh. He's tall, lanky but muscular, like something out of the historical fiction my mother approves in the house. She's against the romanticization of dangers in society, which is what she said when I asked her about ordering more books online. She'd be against Decker, if she knew.

Which is why, of course, I've never breathed a word about him in the six months we've been...talking. At the fence. In midwinter my mother got a cough, and she asked me to take a last-minute delivery to the platform. And there was Decker in an Army-green coat, rubbing his hands together, cheeks pink, watching me. I couldn't help myself. He's got this boyish grin that makes me think of the sunrise, or pulling the ribbon off a gift.

God, I wish I could touch him—and really touch him, not with the cold press of metal against my hips. If I close my eyes and imagine it with all my might, I can almost picture what it would be like to lean my head forward and feel his skin meet mine instead of the frigid kiss of the fence. If I could do that, then I'd know for certain how I felt about him. It's probably love. Love can feel uncertain, can't it? It can feel overwhelming and strange and more than a little dangerous.

"Don't," I whisper back. "My mother…"

He draws back, green eyes instantly knitted. "You changed your mind."

I rub a thumb over the base of his knuckle. "No. God, no." Sparkling adrenaline mixes with breathless heat. "I'm definitely leaving."

Decker blows a breath out through thin lips, slightly chapped from working out in the sun all day. For most of my life I was expressly forbidden from talking to any of the people my mother hired to work in the fields or in the greenhouse. For all her photos cradling the dirt, she doesn't have enough hands to weed, water, and collect her prizewinning blooms. And her flowers do have to be tended, even if she'd rather people think they sprout naturally from the earth, picked with a gentle smile and a thankful prayer by a woman in a linen outfit. The people my mother sells her flowers to desperately want them to be free-range, whatever that means. So she grows them in open fields and a glassed-in greenhouse, scattering the seeds in fistfuls meant to seem random. As if anything my mother ever does is random. Paranoid, yes. Random, no.

But even if she carefully selects every one of those handfuls, it means there are no tidy plots and rows, which would look bad in her brochure photos. It makes no sense. Nobody ever comes here to see what the fields are like. Why would they? She ships the flowers in tightly wrapped Styrofoam coolers to whatever wedding or event they're having—they all go on the train at night. In a few hours, it'll chug to a stop at a wide wooden platform thirty feet beyond where Decker stands at the fence. The night crew will load the coolers on, and they'll be away into the night, the howl of the whistle cutting across the sky to my bedroom window.

Decker leans forward again, angling his face so he can brush his lips against my forehead from the other side. "I've been thinking about us. About being together without this damned fenced in between us."

I pull back an inch, skin bristling. Decker is the first person other than my mother to pay any attention to me, and yet...I'm not entirely certain I like his attention either. I've lived under my mother's thumb every waking hour of my life, even during those three years she let me go to school in the city. She's always watching, always assessing. And I'm always watching her. If I'd done a bad job, she'd never have squeezed my hand. Most nights I dream about wide open fields with no fences and no prying eyes. "Me too," I murmur toward his smile, and then his words settle into my brain."When will everything be ready?"

A broad smile spreads over his face, a strange light in his eyes. "Tonight. We're leaving tonight."

A surge of energy bolts through me from the top of my head to the tips of my toes, the air getting so light it barely fills my lungs. "It's all set?"

"It's all set." Decker leans in hard against the fence and groans. "Christ, I wish I could touch you right now. But soon. When the train comes—" He pulls back to look deeply into my eyes. "You'll be here when the train comes, won't you? You'll meet me tonight?"

"I can get out, but I don't know if I can get back in. If you can't open the gate, if my mother finds me out of the house—"

"It'll be open when you get here, I swear. I have it figured out." Decker laughs, his voice blending with the breeze rustling through the new green leaves. "I have it all figured out." He leans in again, dropping his voice like there might be somebody listening. "By this time tonight, we'll be on our own. I've got you a temporary place to stay in the city—"

"*Us.*"

"I've got *us* a temporary place to stay in the city, one night only, and then we're out of here. It's a wide-open country, Persephone. I can get a job anywhere the road takes us. We could go east, toward the ocean, or into the desert if that's what you want—"

"New York City," I say without pause.

He laughs, because he's heard that before. "Okay, okay. To the library."

"The New York Public Library. With the lions outside." I don't tell him that they're named Patience and Fortitude, those lions. I've waited so long for this chance. I've used all my strength to get here. In some weird way it almost feels like those lions are waiting for me.

"Fine," he says, his tone generous. "We'll head in that direction."

I close my eyes and let the words spin a rose-tinted movie of our new life. One where we'll be able to go to the check out books, an endless amount of books. Oh, god, I know it's going to be hard, leaving everything behind. It's not like my mother has ever let me squirrel money away into a savings account, but I've got a few dollars that Decker's slipped me here and there. And the beginning—well, the beginning of all this does make my stomach clench. But I don't need to focus on the fake ID we'll need to buy if we want to get anywhere without my mother knowing, or the fact that I don't have a credit card. The other girls at school—they all had credit cards. Wasn't much to spend money on while we were on school grounds, but that didn't stop them from buying things. It looked so easy—type in a few numbers, press a button, reinvent yourself. Let people *see* you.

I never did. She'd find out, somehow, the way she found out when we snuck off to have our tarot cards read. The hairs on the back of my neck stand straight up. My mother won't be at the little house Decker and I will set up for ourselves, wherever it is we land. She won't be watching. But he will.

"You can go to work wherever you want, with a face like yours you're bound to get hired. You can wait tables or answer phones." He gives a small laugh. "Maybe even work for a florist."

The snort that escapes me is part excitement and part irritation. Decker has said this a thousand times if he's said it once, and I don't think he knows what he's talking about. "No one's going to hire me for my face." Worry knits my brows. "Will I get hired without references?"

"Of course they will." His fingers curve down over the fence, eyes warm. "You're the most beautiful woman in the world. You're worth a million bucks."

I can't stand it anymore and turn my head, craning my neck to look in every direction. Nothing is out of place at the forest's edge. Sunlight pushes through the leaves like new buds and falls like strings of pearls to the ground below. Bright flowers bow their heads to the wind in a lazy dance. All the growing things fill the air with a green, fresh scent, spring tipping over into summer. Summers will never be the same after this, and I have to admit that part of me aches for these summers already. There is one advantage to having a mother like mine, and it's that she sees the value in lying out in an open field and letting the light soak into your skin. She makes certain allowances, in the summer —like letting me spend an hour alone at the brook on the opposite side of the field, far from the train tracks. In the summer, she likes to pretend that the train and the tracks that jut out of the earth don't exist.

"Did you hear something?" A note of anxiety in Decker's voice.

"Nothing." I take a deep breath and let it out slow. "I should get back, though. She might decide to check on me. If I'm not there, she'll—"

Decker releases me but lets his fingertips hang on the fence for a few heartbeats longer. "You know what time, right? It's important."

This is a risk for both of us. If he gets caught out—with me—he'll never work for my mother again. Knowing her, he might not work anywhere again. I don't want to think about what will happen to me. The doors in our house are made from heavy, solid wood. I'd be no match for a good lock on one of those. But—no need to think of that, because it won't happen. By the time the train comes, she'll be sleeping. She won't know we're gone until it's too late. "I know when the train comes, Deck. I'll be there."

He brings his fingertips to his lips and blows me a kiss. Something flickers across his face. Maybe it's only a shadow from the dappled light. Decker licks his lips and grins at me again. "You're going to feel so good with me, baby. I promise you that."

I let myself believe him, let myself lean hard into what it will be like to belong to him. To belong to anyone, other than my mother. Once we're together, I won't have to be so afraid. I'll love every moment with him. I squeeze my eyes shut and will myself into the future, when he can pull me close and keep me steady while we go out into the world. I'm going to feel so good.

From far off in the distance, somewhere on the other side of the fence, a whistle sounds. That's his cue to go. He looks like he wants to say more, but he only jogs off into the trees, following the tracks.

Tonight.

3

PERSEPHONE

THE FIELDS never seem larger than in the pitch-black of night. This is only the second time I've gone out like this. The first was years ago, back when I'd discovered a slim volume of a ghost story that happened in the New York Public Library. Scary? Creepy, more like. Reading it was like having chill waves of dread lap up against my toes and then my shins and then knees, until it submerged every inch of me. It was about a woman trapped in the library forever--a booklover's dream, maybe. Except there was no light. No electricity. No fire.

No way to read the books.

That might have made me frightened of going to the library, but it only strengthened my determination to leave. At least she had been places before she got trapped. At least she'd read more than a few stolen books. By the time I was done reading it, I had to do something with my pounding heart and the certainty of doom, so I risked it all and went out into the night.

There was nothing in the field, of course. There never is. It's surrounded by high fences, every inch. The house was different then, too. Going out wasn't such a finality.

Still, I walk faster now—as fast as I dare, weaving between the flowers whenever possible. I reach up and touch the flowers still twined into my hair from earlier in the day. It's kind of sweet, to wake up with petals on my pillow, and my mother would have known something was off if I spent a lot of time brushing them away. She'll be apoplectic if I crush the blooms beneath my shoes. There's probably nothing out here now, under the bright swell of the moon, other than stark shadows. Tree branches scrape black against the sky. I'll admit it—I don't want to get too close. Wind rushes by my ears, carrying the creaking of the green-heavy branches. Cicadas sing, jumping out of the way as I go. I'm disturbing them. I'm disturbing myself, but it's the most exhilarating thing I've ever done.

After I read that story the New York Public Library became the symbol of freedom. A lighthouse for me to swim toward when I'm feeling mired in endless flowers. Maybe it won't be impressive at all, but it doesn't matter. It's not about the building. It's not even about the millions of books inside. It's about being the master of my own fate, deciding where I go.

Eventually I have no choice but to head for the forest. The slim line of trees is what separates me from the train, and the train will whisk me away to my new life. I suck in a breath. The air gets more humid by the day. Tomorrow's dewdrops are still hovering in midair. For a moment I see myself the way another person would, with my white dress skimming the grass. I'm a ghost, as insubstantial as a ghost. Any moment now my feet could leave the ground and I could fly off into the sky, dissolving into midnight blue. I wish I had something to carry, other than a small beaded purse, but packing would have given me away. Decker says we can buy everything we need in the city. I was wrong before. I'm *not* ambivalent about him. I was only afraid, and that's not the same thing.

At the tree line I stop one final time. Once I get on the train, there's no going back. A wild instinct bursts out of the cage of my chest—run, run, go home, go back inside, pound on the door, beg her to let me in—but no. I am not a little girl anymore, my mother is not my keeper, and I'm leaving.

I need this.

I fold the purse into the palm of my hand and step into the murky darkness beneath the trees. For the first several paces everything is shadowed, moonlight cutting through the branches and splashing onto the dirt. The shadow changes character as I go, lightening until the soft glow of the streetlamp burns into the night. It's old, the plastic casing around the lightbulb cloudy, but even that much light tells me what I need to know: the fence is open.

The fence is open.

I jump into the air—I can't help it—and come down soft, heat rushing to my cheeks. God, let Decker not have seen me jumping for joy. I don't know who he convinced to give him the key and in this moment I don't care. It's going to be an irrelevant detail in the space of an hour or two. My pulse is a hummingbird, fast and light and giddy. Walk slowly, normally.

The train waits on the tracks.

From my brief stint at boarding school I know what a real train platform is like—I rode this same train into the city, and it let me off at the main station, where a bodyguard my mother hired took me straight to the school's front door. He did more than that, actually. He took me to the door of my bedroom. That man slept in an apartment across the street from the building for three years, watching. My jaw tightens at the memory. I'm just one person. There was never a reason to keep me under lock and key. Nothing ever happened.

Whatever. All of that is in the past. The past, the past, a long time ago. Soon the past will be behind the train, and we'll leave the train behind, and all of this will become like a dream.

The car lined up at the platform has a door flung open wide. From here, it seems like a pitch-dark maw. The gentle rumble of the engine hums underneath the breeze. It's waiting. It's waiting for me.

But where is Decker?

I scan the length of the train, as far as I can see. In the distance another faint light glows, shadows flashing in front of it—they're loading the flowers. Nervousness wraps its hands around my neck. Where is he? We were supposed to meet here.

Maybe he meant *on* the train, not *at* the train. A flush of heat spills down my back. He could be waiting inside for me, hidden from the other men who work on the deliveries, hidden from everyone. For the first time in my life, I don't mind the thought. There won't be any fence inside the train car—just me and Decker, if everything goes according to plan. It's two hours into the city. We could do a lot in two hours.

Don't rush, don't rush. Every instinct says to keep my eyes open, to look around, but I need to listen. I let them flutter closed. Leaves rustle in the wind. Far away, an owl cries. No footsteps, no gasp from my mother—*what are you doing here*? Of course not. She's sleeping, her breathing even and peaceful. Unless she can sense what I'm doing. But that's a ridiculous thought. My mother's not omnipotent. She's just a woman.

Even the dirt beneath my feet has a strange, otherworldly quality. It's been years since I crossed this stretch of ground. I'm going to need new shoes in the city, I know that already—the soft canvas ones won't last long on paved roads.

Why doesn't he come out and lean against the door, that familiar grin on his face?

Maybe he's preparing a surprise.

I can't stop my own grin from taking over. Surprises—I love surprises. At least, I think I do, in theory. I've read about them in books. A crowd of people behind a door ready to shout *happy birthday*. A gift presented with a shy flourish. My god, he *is*. Decker is exactly the kind of person who will know how important this is, and I bet he's going to give me my first real surprise. I'm sure he's that kind of person. He's never seemed to be anything else, and we've talked every day for months.

There's still no sign of him as I take the last few steps to the train car. A set of steps leads into the inside. The handle is cold under my palm. I heave myself up, ready to pass out from the anticipation. It might not be so bad to tumble into Decker's arms and wake up in a new life.

But the train car is dark.

Of course it's dark—I would have seen light coming from the inside, obviously. Obviously. But it's *completely* dark, not a single running light on. My eyes adjust bit by bit.

It's not a special train car.

I shake off the disappointment like an errant fall of raindrops. I don't know why I expected it to be a special car. This isn't a first-class trip to the city, it's a midnight escape. Still, this is... it's nothing. It's clean, yes. Enough light comes in through a narrow window at the very front of the car to see a pair of seats, more of a bench, against the back wall. The rest is empty space. This is a storage car, not one of the passenger cars.

I swallow hard, shame pummeling my disappointment. I didn't come here for luxury, I came here to get out. And this is going to be our *life*. Decker can't afford a fancy house, but at least he can accept it graciously. He's not worried about paying for everything—about starting our new life with the little we've managed to scrape up without attracting attention. He's not longing for piles of money or an extravagant lifestyle. Neither am I.

One last scan of the car. Where is he? Goosebumps crawl up the flesh of my arms and down my spine.

"Decker?" It takes everything in me to get the word out, and it's barely above a whisper. I clear my throat and try again. "Deck, are you here?"

If I'm too loud, somebody else running beside the train for the night shift could hear me. I'd never forgive myself if I got all this way only to screw it up by shouting for Decker. I just want to know he's *here.* More than I want the train to finally pull away. More than I want to leave it behind in the city. My skin heats with wanting. Where is he, where is he?

A sound like someone being sick wriggles into the train car.

It's so soft that I dismiss it as noise from the forest. There are a hundred things moving and living out there. Any one of them could have made a strange noise.

It happens again.

The other door out of this train car is up in the front, by the narrow window. Clouded glass keeps me from seeing out, even with my face pressed against the surface. I try the handle. The door opens without a sound.

One step out onto the connector, and I wish I'd never come.

The air is a knife against my skin, sharp and cold. My stomach twists. Shock bores in behind my eyes and squeezes, viselike and terrible, so strong I have to clutch the handle on the side of the train to stay upright.

I've found Decker.

Now the sound makes sense. It wedges itself into my understanding.

Decker's feet are feet six inches off the ground in the center of the clearing, kicking uselessly into the open air. It should be impossible. He's too tall to have his feet so far off the ground. He's too tall, but the man holding him there is taller. *Bigger.* And infinitely stronger.

I've never seen Luther Hades. But I don't need a photo ID to know it's him.

Only Luther Hades could suck all the light from around him, turning moonlight into dark. Only Luther Hades could look that huge, or that lethal.

Only he could make Decker, who reminds me of a tall tree, look small.

The biggest dog I've ever seen sits at Hades' feet, fur darker than the night around them, growling at Decker but staying still. For now. We're surrounded by death, aren't we? My mother never mentioned anything about a dog, but there it is, tensed, waiting. Not tied to anything. It could do *anything*. It's as dangerous as he is. As deadly. They're a matched set, taking up all the space in the world.

A memory screeches across the back of my brain—a photograph, shoved into my face, my mother saying *if you see a man who looks like this, you run, you run as fast as you can. You scream.* I see him now, feet planted in the earth. I'd know his face anywhere. I was born to know his face, to run from it. But I can't run now. I can't move. *Where did she get that picture?* It doesn't matter, it doesn't matter. All those things might as well be buried underground.

Because it's really him, it's really the man who wants to kill me—the moonlight shows me a sharp silhouette of his face, and I can't look away.

He's got his hands around Decker's throat.

He's choking him to death.

4

HADES

My first impression of her, out of the corner of my eye and bleached by moonlight, is that Demeter has been hiding an angel. Not just a daughter, but a creature of sky and air. No one appears out of darkness so brightly, like a light source is beneath her skin and woven in with the fabric of her dress. The breeze picks up the hem and plays with it. The motion hooks me in the center of my chest. One glance, and the man wriggling beneath my hands is nothing to me. He's always been nothing, from the moment he walked up to the door of my train car and stepped in like he owned it.

Mistake.

I relished his expression—shock, turning to horror

while my dog Conor put his body between us with a vicious growl, showing off for me—for a full five heartbeats before I dragged him back outside, Conor following at my feet, wary and watching. Nothing interested me less than his sputtered excuses about *meeting someone else* and *I didn't expect* and *please, I'll just* and so on. I got tired of it soon enough. Anyone unintelligent enough to climb onto random train cars with the swagger of my older brother runs the risk of paying the price, and tonight the price is that I'm slowly cutting off his air supply. The man is weak. Betrayal made him this way. For all his fieldwork muscles, he's absolutely incapable of doing anything. His hands scrabble weakly at my wrists. He is nothing.

And now he's less than nothing, because I can't look away from the woman standing on the connector between two train cars, her hands to her mouth, eyes wide and horrified. The dress—it reminds me of Demeter in the way it performs simplicity. That woman is anything but simple. This woman, I can tell, is the third rail. In the moonlight I see every detail and envy tears through me.

I'm jealous of the moonlight touching her skin.

I'm only touching this wriggling fish of a man.

A siren sounds in the back of my mind, struggling to override the powerful urge to snap his neck and get my hands on her as quickly as possible. *There will be consequences*, the voice of reason howls. *Look at her, look at her—*

I *am* looking at her. Conor looks, too, with a low, questioning growl.

"Stay."

He stays. He always does. When he was a puppy, I spent hours shaping him into the guard dog he would become. Those hours pay off especially well in moments like this, when I want people shaken to the core.

White dress, hair spilling down her back in curls, the gentle slope of her waist up to perfect tits. What's under the dress, aside from those tits? Little to nothing, judging by the hard little peaks of her nipples.

I want her.

My mind sighs with all the things I could do to that pretty little body, consequences be damned. I shove the idea of the apocalypse, of all these fields burning around me, out of my mind, crushing it under one foot like a spent cigarette. Fuck all of that. What matters now, in the wordless animal part of me, are all the sensations crashing together in a hail of lust. My blood unleashed, thundering through my veins. The tease of the night breeze on my skin. And the pulse between my legs, harder than iron.

A movement distracts me, a glancing blow against my shin. It's so pathetic it might as well be the touch of a tailor, whisper-light. But it reminds me that I'm currently killing a man who has gone horribly off-course. I waste a look on him. The moonlight leeches his skin of color, but I can still see the dusky shade to his cheeks. Might as well end it now so I can turn my attention to better things. I didn't need him anyway.

"Stop." Her clear, young voice rings like a bell across the space between us. "Please."

I'm watching his eyes, not hers, but that *please* lights up kindling at the base of my spine. That—I want more of *that*. The edge of fear, the end of the word almost, almost, slipping into a whimper. I'm torn. I want to see her face when she begs, but something interesting happens when she does it—the half-dead man's eyes open wide. His expression, for someone on the brink, has an element of hope. A little more of it, a little brighter, would make it even more of a pleasure when I stamp it out. I could say *yes.* "No."

She leaves the train with footfalls soft as rain.

"You're killing him." Her half-exhaled words are thick with desperation and tears. I want to lick those tears away from her skin, more than I've ever wanted anything. No wonder Demeter kept her hidden. No wonder, no wonder. To think of what a man could do to her.

Ah—that's it, isn't it? This man, the one who couldn't even enter a train and escape with his life—he had plans for her. No doubt she believed whatever pretty things he said to her. Boys like this, with smiles like that, are all talk, the fuckers.

"That's right. I *am* killing him."

"No, please—please don't do that." She can hardly draw a full breath, and the sound of it is intoxicating. I reward myself with a glance. Tears stream silently down her cheeks. "I know who you are. Don't do this."

A laugh tumbles out from between my lips before I

can stop it. "You know who I am. So? Why should I spare your boyfriend?"

She hesitates. That moment of hesitation confirms what I already knew—this is Demeter's daughter, without a shadow of a doubt. This innocent creature, the one her mother named Persephone, radiating innocence and terror, actually fucking *hesitates*.

"He's not my boyfriend. We've never—we didn't say that we were together. We were going to—" He couldn't even convince her that they were in love. Something less than a man sags in my grip. I'll give him this—he fought longer than I expected to. But she's delivered a killing blow.

"You were going to meet him, weren't you? Out in the middle of the night, all alone. And then what?"

"Go to the city." A mournful half-sob. "Then go somewhere else, somewhere my mother couldn't find us."

That sparks my interest. A girl like this, thinking she's running away from Demeter? A very interesting choice, though of course that's not what the fool in my hands had in mind. What he had in mind was a double-cross. I could laugh.

But Persephone. Why would she want to leave all that power behind? Unless, of course, she didn't have access to it. But why wouldn't she? Demeter will need a successor eventually. In her line of work, most people don't grow very old.

"That's not going to happen now," I tell her casually. "You must know that."

"Why not?" Such an adorable struggle. She clearly doesn't want to sound plaintive, and yet...she does. "You could let him go." In my peripheral vision I see her hands lift, then fall helplessly back to her sides. "If you let us go we would never bother you again."

"You won't bother me again anyway." I'm committed. I want the adrenaline and the release. The world will never miss a nobody like the one I've caught. "Really, you should be grateful."

"Grateful for what?" Persephone comes a tentative step forward.

"That I let you watch. If you hurry, you might even get to say goodbye."

I've been toying with the bastard. One swift snap and this is all over. The summer wind kicks up and the train whistle wails across the night, setting Persephone into motion.

She runs across the empty space and throws herself against my arm, her legs pressed against Conor's side. He snaps at her, growling, and a bark tears loose into the air—but he doesn't move except for the trembling of his body. He holds himself back, even though nobody runs at him that way. Nobody runs at *me* that way. And here she is, ready to get torn apart.

"*Down.*" Conor backs off, but he's not happy about it. Tension pours off of him, but he puts his head down on his hands. He trembles almost as much as she does. A cool wash of adrenaline spills into my veins, probably from shock. She isn't strong enough to pull my arms away from her boyfriend or break my grip, and after a moment I realize through her sobs that she's not trying to. She's only trying to get my attention.

He makes a horrible sound, halfway under the ground already, and Persephone gasps the sharp gasp of all women since time immemorial.

"*Please,*" she cries. "Don't kill him. There must be something I can do, something—"

Oh, the sweet thing. I look down at her, clinging ineffectually to my arm. Nothing would be better than to let her think she's coming with me of her own free will. Nothing in the world.

"I'm not here to make a bargain."

Her eyes are huge and dark, tears glistening on her chin. She licks her lips.

"I'll do anything."

In that moment something shifts, a boulder rolling away from the open mouth of a cave, dawn splitting the sky above. I'm taking her regardless. The world has presented me with an opportunity and I'm seizing it, whether that opportunity fights me or not. But the tears, and the begging, and the noble sacrifice—I want more of that, too. And I fucking shouldn't. I absolutely shouldn't. I should kill the man as an object lesson in being more careful and let her run back to her mother's house.

I let the fool in my hands fall to the ground.

It's a sudden drop and he has no time to catch himself. The guy's body spills onto the dirt in a heap. Is he breathing? I don't know, and I don't care.

Persephone lets go of my arm, a fresh wave of sobs, the pitch rising.

Conor gets to his feet.

I put a hand on his head. "Wait. You might still get your chance."

He makes an impatient sound.

"Decker," she gasps, and I roll my eyes. *Decker*. Not *my love*, not *darling*, not any other term of endearment. Just her ticket out. And here she is, fluttering around him like they're Romeo and Juliet.

"Deck, wake up." He coughs once and rolls over onto his side, knees folding up into the fetal position. Pity. Persephone falls to her knees and puts a hand on his cheek. "Oh, I thought, I thought—I love you, I thought it was too late—"

She *loves* him now. How precious.

One sharp whistle and shadows detach from the trees. The train howls out its own whistle a second time. The train won't actually leave until I tell it to, but she doesn't need to know that. I pluck her up by the waist, practically weightless, and she tries to get back down.

"No, *no*, let me go—"

This puts Conor on edge. He nudges my shin, baring his teeth. He wants a piece of her. I want a piece of her too.

I slip one hand around her throat. Fuck, she's delicate, her pulse fluttering just underneath the skin. Persephone goes still and lets me turn her to face me. She pants as I run the pad of my thumb over her chin. It quivers, trembling along with the rest of her body.

"Are you going to kill me now?"

My men step up behind her, but she doesn't dare turn her head. Two of them hook their arms under Decker's and drag him past us, giving us a wide berth. Her eyes follow his slumped body. The man won't shut up. All the groaning, the whining—fucking pathetic.

"You said you would do anything to save him. That was your bargain. Are you telling me you'd rather be dead?"

A flicker of fear is chased off her face by a nameless expression, a light flaring in her eyes. She glances down at Conor, the whites of her eyes glowing in the moonlight. “No,” she whispers. “I want to live.”

I lean in close, bending down so my lips are level with her ear. Her heart beats hard under my fingertips. She smells sweet, like roses and sunshine and something unique to her. It must be the fresh softness of her. Fuck, the things I’m going to do to her, dangling her not-boyfriend on a string as if she’ll ever be anything but mine. The urge to throw her down into the dirt is so strong it almost overtakes me, but now that all this has transpired, it’s best for the train to move on. I’m no longer interested in dealing with Demeter tonight—not now that I have her daughter for my very own.

The poor thing.

“We’ll see how long that lasts.”

5

PERSEPHONE

I SHOULD SCREAM and kick and pound at his back. I should fight him or die trying. There are lots of things I should do.

But the one thing my mother never explicitly warned me about—god, she never told me anything, it's clear, it's *so* clear—is that he's huge. He's not just ruthless. He's not just strong. He's taller than Decker by a good five inches, and the two of them together—

I choke back a sob. Decker never stood a chance. I've never seen muscles on a man like this before, and the only men I've ever really seen are my mother's fieldworkers. None of them look this strong. None of them *feel* this strong. He's got an iron grip just under my ass and I don't even have to struggle to know that I'll never, never get free. The dream of seeing the New York Public Library—gone up in flames. Cicadas scream on my behalf.

The night breeze is the world's gentlest caress on my skin, not even powerful enough to dry my tears. So I let them fall to the ground behind us. My heart could stop right this instant. It hurts like a broken rib. I've never been so far over my head in my life. *I'll do anything.* That's what I said, and I saw it in Luther Hades' eyes—the moment he accepted the deal. There was no relief there, or happiness. Only a cruel satisfaction. What else was I supposed to do? What else was I supposed to do? Let Decker die? And what does it mean that the smallest, worst part of me considered it?

But I didn't run, did I? No. I traded the only thing I have to give. *Me.* And I might not know much about the world, but I know this—people live and die by vague terms. Maybe that was why she said the same thing about Hades over and over again. *If he finds you, he will kill you.*

She was wrong about that.

He hasn't killed me.

Not yet.

And whatever happens now could be far, far worse.

I want to howl for Decker, to chase after the men until they let me see if he's all right. My chest aches with suppressing a ragged shout. He's not all right. How could he be all right? How could he ever be all right again?

How could *I*?

Hades cuts off my thoughts with an abrupt turn, his dog padding quietly along next to his feet. It's a massive dog, sharp-teeth, and I heard its growl. I couldn't say what kind it is but I don't need to know. It could kill me as easily as Hades could, but there's only so much room for fear in my head. All of it blends together, loud and pounding.

We're only one car back from the car I came through, but it might as well be a hundred miles. I pick my head up and crane my neck for a glimpse of Decker. The retreating shadows of the men who dragged him away grow dimmer in the far distance. Another cascade of sobs falls from my lips. I gulp them back and Hades laughs, the low rumble soft against my belly through his shoulders.

"Don't hold back." His arm tightens across my legs. "I'm very much enjoying the sound of your tears. It's such a..." He cocks his head to the side, leaving a bare inch of space for the night to rush into. "It's such a pure sadness. Lovely."

"You're horrible," I choke out, and then I'm falling, moving so fast I can't help bracing for the impact that's sure to come.

It never does. Instead, Hades sets me on my feet on the top step of the train car. My knees wobble. I hope, I pray, that the dress is hiding it. He considers me from a few steps away. Silhouetted there in the moonlight, all of him stands out in sharp relief—only something's different, something's wrong. The way the shadows play over his face isn't quite right, like he's pulling the moonlight into his own dark heart and stripping all the brightness away. The light can only get as close as the edges of him, and then... somehow, he repels it. My own breath sounds harsh and loud against the hum of the train and the wash of the wind in the leaves.

"Would a horrible man be so kind to you?" A grin flashes across his face, teeth white in the strange shadows. He radiates a mean confidence. It comes off him in waves. *The city has violence.* This *man* has violence. His dog paws at the ground. "I've even left the flowers in your hair."

"If you were being kind you would have killed me already." He's torturing me now without touching me. A better man wouldn't put me through this crushing terror, but he loves it. An unspeakable fear closes my throat. The wondering tone about the flowers is scarier than everything else.

"I'm honoring your own request." He puts his hands in his pockets, standing tall. Hades takes a single step forward, but it's like he's slammed a door on the rest of the world. "If I recall correctly, you were willing to trade anything to save that young man's life. It's a fair trade, don't you think? Your life for his?"

"So you *are* going to kill me." My chin shakes, and damn it, if I have to die, I don't want to do it with a quivering chin and a snotty nose. "Just do it then."

Hades tips his head back and laughs. It's the most terrifying sound I've ever heard, and yet—and yet—something about it strikes me as absolutely beautiful. It fits him, even while it gets under my skin, down to the bones. He raises one hand and I grit my teeth. I'm not going to take a step back. I don't even know if I can take a step back, but I'm not going to. I lift my chin, making room for his hand around my throat, and he makes a soft *mmm* sound.

"You're offering," he muses. "Either you're hoping I kill you, or you're doing your best to meet the terms of our little arrangement." His hand hovers in the air, close enough for me to feel the heat of his palm but not touching me—not yet. "Of course, there's another explanation for baring that pretty neck to me."

He lets the statement hang in the air until I'm ready to burst. The train whistle sounds again—this is the third time—but Hades doesn't so much as blink. He's watching me. It's more than watching, though —this is no casual gaze. He's pinning me here with his eyes. Making me wait. Stripping me down. Heat sears across my cheeks. I'll do anything, I'd said. I expected him to kill us both, honestly. I believed my mother. I was willing to throw myself onto the sword to save Deck, or at least die with him, and now— I clear my throat so I can force the words out.

"There's no other explanation."

"You don't want to admit that you want this." I

shake my head, horrified. No, no, *no*. "Oh, not on the surface, sweetheart. Deep down, where you feel the most filthy and dirty and shameful. I think that part of you likes a hand on your throat. I'm not surprised, given the company you've been keeping."

My lips have gone numb, but even worse, the heat has fled my cheeks and gone down between my legs. Hot shame presses my thighs together.

"I was trying to survive. I only wanted—"

"I like it when you cry." Hades does touch me now, two fingertips on my cheek, burning a path along the tracks of my tears. "I like the way it makes your body shake. A man could get drunk off that feeling."

I press my lips together, trying not to let any more tears leak out. It's a futile thing. I couldn't stop them if I tried.

"That's what you want from me?"

"I don't want anything from you." Hades presses one thick finger to my lips, silencing me. My breath superheats in my lungs. I have a chestful of shame. *He's right*, that little voice taunts. *He's right, and you know it.* "It's not about wanting, it's about *taking*. And

I'm going to take everything you offered." He cocks his head to the side, studying my lips. "You know, not many men would let you buy something as *valuable* as a life without upfront payment. Luckily for you, I have a sense of honor. Turn around."

The air rushes out of my lungs in a whoosh.

"What?" He makes me say it against his finger.

Hades leans in. "Turn around."

A montage of terrible things stampedes through my mind. Now? Here? On the steps of a train car? It's too much, too soon, and at the same time I'm seized with a desire so powerful the hairs on the back of my arms stand up. The anticipation is always the worst part. I've learned that enough times, living with my mother. If he'd only just start, if he'd only just do what he's going to do, I could finally exhale. But I can't, because I'm frozen here on the steps, his eyes concealed by the thickening night, and if there's one thing I do know, it's this—you don't turn your back on the monster in the room. I *won't* turn my back on the dog, which looks ready to attack. It reminds me of Hades. They're too similar. Too big and terrifying.

Hades drops his hand.

"You're slow to obey, I see. That won't be a problem for very long."

"I—" There's nothing I can say to that. He looks like he could stand at the bottom of the stairs forever and never get tired. There's no choice but to do what he says. And in fact, I agreed to it—I did. I made a deal. I said anything. Whatever Hades is planning now is part of anything. Why, why, why was I so careless? Would Decker have done the same for me?

It dawns, slowly—maybe he *did* do the same for me. Maybe he was trying to put himself on the line, trying to distract Hades, and that's what I interrupted. Decker was not dead when they took him away. There's still hope he's alive now. But I saw Hades' hands around his neck. I saw the casual way he stood. It wasn't an effort for him, killing Decker—it would have been easy, and he would have gone on with his life as if nothing had happened. I'm the only thing standing in the way of that now. I don't know where they've taken Decker but this, tonight, this is proof that it doesn't matter. My mother was right. Hades will find him and kill him, and that will be the end of the game. I owe him. A full-body shudder moves through me. I have to do this, and I have to do it now.

"T-turn around and do what?"

Another slow smile, the hint of a laugh. I hold my breath, the pressure of the air around me pressing in on my head and on my heart and on the sick desire knotting in my belly.

"It's not obvious? Don't lie to me." Hades puts his fingers beneath my chin and moves my head back and forth, watching, watching. "I liked it when you lied before, even while you pressed those thighs together and pretended you don't feel it. But don't do it now. I'll know, and then you'll have to pay the price."

"It's not obvious," I blurt, I beg. "What do you want me to do?"

"Turn around," he says again. "And get on the fucking train."

6

PERSEPHONE

THE OUTSIDE of the train car gave nothing away, its shell the same black, sleek exterior as the other cars. I edge into Hades' train car sideways, breath shallow. I don't want to turn all the way around. If I take my eyes off him, god knows what he'll become. He's already the worst thing I could imagine.

It's not his looks that make my knees weak, it's how he had Decker—strong, capable Decker—in midair without so much as breaking a sweat. Or maybe it *is* his looks. I don't know anymore. My brain is nothing. My brain is the breeze in the leaves—leaves I might never see again.

He steps into the car behind me, his frame filling the door. For an instant I think he might not make it through. Then he angles his shoulders, the movement graceful and controlled, and I have to scoot out of the way so he can rise to his full height behind me.

I don't mean to stare, but in the warm, golden light of the train car, I... have no other choice.

Hades is exactly as tall and broad as he was outside, only more so now that we're in an enclosed space. My brain struggles to put all the pieces of him together at once. I wasn't wrong about the way the light reacts to him. He wears a rich charcoal suit that might as well be a black hole. There's not a hint of shine to it, like the suit jacket I found at the back of my mother's closet once upon a time. At boarding school I picked up enough fashion knowledge to know that this is no off-the-rack garment. It was made for him.

And the body underneath the suit—

Flawless. I press my thighs together again at the sight of him. Decker has a rough-and-tumble attractiveness, some muscles bigger than others, nothing quite matching up. But Luther Hades looks like he was born to wear expensive suits as much as he was born to throw me over his shoulder. Everything about him is symmetrical, perfect. The suit slides over hard biceps and I bet if I pulled his shirt out of his pants and looked underneath—

I bet—

Oh, god, I can't even think of it. I bet he'd still be perfect. I swallow hard. All the books I've read, I realize now, are complete fantasies. In real life, men as evil as Hades don't have to have an outward mark to tell you that they're the devil. Hades certainly doesn't. *This is a man*, I think wildly. *This is a real man.* I try to bat the thought away, but it seems so real and foundational and true. I gave up my life for Decker, but I never once felt lightheaded at the sight of him.

A jagged tear appears in my mind. Everything about his clothes and his train car is supposed to be about refinement. But all I can feel is the violence coiled underneath all that fine fabric. His clothes don't hide it. They *enhance* it. He could kill wearing the most expensive piece of clothing I've ever seen.

Hades snaps his fingers in front of my eyes.

I blink up at him, breath stopping again at the sight of his face. His face. His body is one thing, but his face—I've never seen any man so cruelly beautiful.

Pale blue eyes like chips out of the springtime sky. Sandy hair, catching the golden light in short glossy strands. He looks out at me, cheekbones sharp enough to cut, and a perfectly cruel jaw.

"Ah—so you *do* like what you see." His lips curve upward in something between a sneer and a smile. "But I didn't tell you to stare. I told you to get on the train."

"No, I—" *Yes.* I do like it. I can't help it. He's beautiful and his clothes are beautiful and this train car is everything I was hoping for out there in the woods, back when I was still a fool. "It's hard to look away."

Behind him, the door slides shut. He slaps a palm to the wall beside him. It glows, then fades away, and the train starts moving. My balance is off on my wobbly knees and I fall sideways, unceremonious, one palm thrown out to stop my fall—but I never hit the floor. Hades catches me around the waist again. I feel the place where he's touching me over my entire side, like an electric current.

"Pay attention," he growls. "If you hit your head on the furniture, you won't be of any use to me." He wraps his other huge hand around my waist and pushes me backward. This time, the landing is a soft one—plush and overstuffed, actually. It does nothing to calm me. His dog is instantly between us, guarding, watching me. The beginnings of a growl rumble in his throat. *Wolf.* He's more like a wolf—too big and powerful to be a pet.

"Conor." Hades snaps his fingers, and it's like I never existed—either to him or to the dog. There's enough light here to see that Conor is the color of midnight and *strong*, not an ounce of extra fat on him. He crosses the train car, nails clicking on the floor, and curls up in front of the fireplace. The *fireplace.* A low fire burns in a grate by the train's outer wall.

I have the distinct sensation of the sun going behind a cloud. It makes no sense, because if anyone was ever the opposite of the sun, it's Hades. He's not the sun, and he's not the moon. He is total darkness, a place no light can touch.

He moves through the train car, stopping to pat Conor's head, which gives me a moment to catch my breath. Then he stands at the edge of a desk that's clearly been made to fit him—sturdy and gleaming polished wood, a deep, dark color with a hint of red. He removes one cufflink, then the other, and drops them both on the surface of the desk with a muffled metallic click. The desk must be bolted to the floor. Everything in here must be bolted to the floor, because it all sways with the movement of the train. Although...something is different. It would have been a different ride in the dusty interior of the next car up on that hard bench. This car must've been built to his specifications, so that Hades, the man I've sworn to do anything for, moves in complete comfort. Every detail could have sprung from his bones, fully formed. The rich paneling on the walls. Deep green-gray furniture, the hue of the summer grass at night. He turns from his desk and undoes the buttons of his jacket, then slips it from his shoulders. My heart stops, then stutters to a start.

Behind the desk is a door. Past the door is the corner of a bed, done up in sheets the color of his suit. My stomach clenches, and I dig one hand into the armrest on this—what is it? A small sofa.

Hades pauses by a set of built-in cabinets and touches one of the slats. It rolls up to reveal a full bar—glasses and bottles of alcohol. My mother only ever kept wine in the house, and this—this is not wine. The amber liquids are in unmarked bottles. I bet he has that specially made, too.

He pours himself a glass like I'm not even there, then turns around and watches me while he sips it.

"Still paying attention?"

"Yes." I sit up straight. It's sick, how hard I've been trying to do what he said. How hard I've been paying attention to this man, and his dog, both of whom could be the end of me right now. All it would take is one decision from him. A snap of his fingers.

I don't want him to make me wish I was dead, I really don't. I don't want him to be the man I know he is. And some small part of me knows that even if I obey him flawlessly, it will never, ever change him. I didn't come here to change him. I came here to pay what I owe. Tears fill my eyes again at the thought of Decker's body dangling uselessly in the air, his feet kicking more slowly with every second. "I'm paying attention."

"Good. Then we'll begin."

I lick at suddenly dry lips, folding my hands into my lap. Oh god, oh *god*. I thought I'd talked myself down from the panic before but it rises again, thick and suffocating. A thousand questions come to mind and die on the tip of my tongue.

Hades sits on the wider sofa across the train car, feet planted on the ground, glass cupped in the palm of his hand. He takes a sip and surveys me, eyes cold. A shiver crawls down my spine. My heart kicks up, thrashing around inside my rib cage, screaming to get out. Just start already, please, please, *please.* I open my mouth to let the plea slip out into the air, but Hades speaks first.

"Come here."

Already, the sofa has come to represent the safest place in the room. As if a piece of furniture could stop him from coming over here himself. A firework exploding, sending shards of shame through every part of me, and I get to my feet. My knees start up again, going loose and useless, and I have to lock them to stay upright. *Don't faint.* I unlock them, rocking them forward an inch. Just move.

I take the first step, and Hades holds up a hand.

"Not like that, sweetheart."

I don't know what he means. There's no other way to get across the floor except for walking.

Unless—

I don't know what he means, and then suddenly, awfully, I do.

"I—I'm wearing a dress."

A glint sparks in his eyes, and I want to clap a hand over my mouth. I'm already here because of my reckless words, and now I'm going to end up without a dress. He'll see everything. The linen tank I have a hundred of. *Had.* The—the white panties. Oh, god, *no*. And on top of this—on top of it all—I have to crawl past the dog with the scariest teeth on the planet. Conor.

"So you *do* understand." He laughs, that same sound that burns my cheeks. "Come here."

I drop to my knees onto the plush carpeting, which still carries the scent of a lightly perfumed cleaner, something meant to evoke clean laundry. It works, and before I can stop myself I've dug my hands into it, eyes burning.

"Don't hide your tears." I look up into Hades' face, and his intense gaze is changed, brightened. He's enjoying this. "I want to see them all. Keep that pretty chin up while you crawl to me."

My hands are cement blocks, my knees totally ineffectual, but I put one palm after the other, one knee after the other, while hot tears slip down. At the last moment he points between his legs. I'll never make it. I'll never be able to make myself do this—not with humiliation sloshing against every last inch of me.

And the most humiliating thing of all?

It's not every last inch.

Because between my legs, desire builds with every sway of my hips and every press of my palms into the carpet.

I stop between his wide legs, looking up at him, trying to keep my breathing even. Hades reaches down and puts a hand under my chin, jerking my head up another inch, peering down at me. That filthy, hidden part of me sighs with relief even as the rest of me recoils. I have to let him do this—for Decker. But I cannot feel this way about it. I can't.

Hades looks down at me and smiles, and I can't tell which parts of me have gone cold and which parts have gone hot. All I know is that I want him to let go, to let *me* go. Yes. That's what I want. That's what I need, and I don't need anything else.

"You took too long, but you get extra points for crying. I fucking love that." His teeth scrape at his bottom lip.

"Can I go back to the sofa now?" Another tear works its way free, my heart throbbing. This is enough for now. It has to be enough for now.

"Do you really think I'm done with you? Tell the truth." The simple words might as well be curses. He leans down, the scent of him surrounding me. "Tell me now."

"No," I choke out. "I didn't think—I only thought, since—"

"Shut your pretty little mouth."

I snap my lips closed.

"I'm not done with you now, and I'll never be done with you. Those are the terms in exchange for your piece of shit boyfriend's life. You did it, Persephone. You saved him. But you'll never save yourself." He lifts me up by the chin, quickly enough that I have to scramble to my feet. He holds me off-balance, leaning close, and I want to collapse into him and sob against his shirt. It's sick, it's wrong, I want it.

The train carries me away from my mother's house, away from everything I've ever known, at a break-neck pace. My mind breaks away, going back to those fields. I hated the fences. I might love them now.

He snaps his fingers in front of my eyes again, the sound startling me.

"Now." It's all I can do to stay upright, even with his hand gripping my chin. "Let's find out what else you'll do."

7

PERSEPHONE

I TREMBLE IN HIS HANDS, and Hades watches this as dispassionately as you'd watch a flower grow. Unlike my mother, he wouldn't think twice about crushing them under his heel, or in his hands. He'd just as soon tear out the petals and spit on them.

"The crawling was fine." A cold assessment. The way you'd talk about a *thing*. "The tears are delicious, but you'll have to do better than that."

He rises to his feet, towering over me. I just can't move. I can't anticipate what he'll do or what he'll say, so I stand there, rooted to the spot, staring at the buttons on his dress shirt. It's the nicest dress shirt I've ever seen. Some of the other girls at school had spare clothes aside from the uniforms, and I could tell those dresses cost a lot—but this? It's nicer than all of them combined.

"Mmm. I have to say, Persephone, the sight of you scared..." He makes a low noise in the back of his throat. "You were such a courageous little thing out there, offering yourself up." He laughs again, and I want to sink down to the floor and hide my face. Even more than that, I want to hook my fingers in the space between the buttons of his shirt and hold on for dear life.

"I'm not afraid of you. I've known you were dangerous all my life. That—that doesn't make me afraid." I have never been so terrified. It's become the air I breathe and the rise and fall of my lungs.

"It's strange that you didn't warn your boyfriend about me, given all that you know about me." His eyes rake across my face. My lips. My neck.

"He's not my boyfriend. I said that before."

His bristling silence tells me I've stepped in the direction of defiance, and the air crackles with a warning. "So you don't *really* care whether he lives or dies"

I look up into his face, as best I can from this distance.

"That's not true. I—I love him." It's not true, and a flash in Hades' eyes tells me he believes it as much as I do. "We weren't together like that. My mother would never have let me be with him. It was something we were going to discuss when we got to the city."

"Oh, isn't that sweet." He clicks his tongue. "You should be thanking me. I've saved you from a lifetime of cooking his dinners and pretending to be interested."

I press my lips closed. Terror mixes with confusion, all of it wrapped in the overpowering need to survive. I *did* love Decker. I loved him enough to try to save him from Hades. But something rings terribly true in Hades' words, all of it shaking the foundations of me like a two-ton bomb. Is he right, or am I just so afraid that I'm taking his word for it? Why would I take Luther Hades' word for anything? And yet that's exactly what I've done.

"I wasn't pretending." Some part of me *was* pretending, but which part? The girl who had never had a boyfriend before, pretending to know what she was doing? Or the woman who had fallen in love, pretending it wasn't happening?

"Good. Prove it to me." He takes me by the arm and turns me to face the desk. "Bend over the desk." He puts a hand on the back of my neck. "You had so much trouble understanding my instructions before, so I'll make it easy. Bend."

I can't breathe. I can't think. I can only obey. I thought crawling was the worst of it, I thought the nightmarish images that came to mind about what men do to women were the worst of it—I never—I *never*—the desk meets my hips; a hard, unforgiving line. I'm painfully aware of the curve of my back and my ass and then the press of my breasts against the unyielding surface.

"What are you going to do?" I whisper. "Please, tell me."

He gives my neck a shake and my cheek makes contact with the desk.

"A summary of my plans for you isn't part of the terms." Another shake, harder. "In fact, I've already held up my end of the deal." Hades rubs a thumb absently up and down the side of my neck, underneath my hair, then lets go. "I didn't kill that disgusting worm of a man. I didn't kill you, though... I could." My body fights between tensing up and giving in to the slow slide of his thumb. Why, *why*, would I ever want to let that relax me? It's not me wanting it, I decide. It's my traitor of a body. "You're so small. It would be nothing."

The heat of my cheek has already warmed up the desk beneath it.

"I thought you wanted me alive." I keep my eyes firmly focused on the shuttered window on the opposite side of the train. The thought of him seeing me like this, bent like this—it can't get any worse.

It gets worse.

"I'll get considerably more enjoyment out of a live woman than a dead one." The hand lifts from the back of my neck, but I stay pressed flat against the desk. He hasn't said to get up. Hades makes a satisfied clicking sound. "Look at you, trying to anticipate my wishes. Can you anticipate what will happen to you next?"

My breath stops, and there it is, that damn chin going again. A million images run through my mind. A million horrible, filthy images, snapshots of things depraved people would do. I—I know that not all sex is bad, but most of it must be. My mother kept all of it from me for a reason. And the things the other girls talked about at school were nothing like this. They involved soccer players and football captains and coaches, not bending over a desk, ass lifted up toward a man who'd just as soon kill me as—

"No," I breathe. "I don't know."

"You're lying." He kicks my legs apart, and it's only then that I realize I've pinned them together as tightly as the muscles will allow. "You might wear a white dress and live on your mother's farm, but she'll have told you things."

"No." Desperation rises in another round of tears and they drip down onto the polished surface below my face. "She's never told me anything—anything about this, about—about any of that."

His hand slips down my spine, counting each ridge, until he stops just above the swell of my ass.

"You bleed every month without knowing why?"

"I know why." I'm incandescent with shame. How can he say all this out into the open air? "I know about...getting pregnant." The warm air from the train car slips underneath the hem of my dress and strokes me between my legs, where all that separates me from Hades is a thin layer of cotton.

This conversation is beyond the pale. Every movement in the air, every movement of his hand—all of them are magnified, intensified. A whisper of air, of breath, and then—the hem of my dress lifts.

Every inch. I feel every inch of my legs as he exposes them, little by little, torturing me. The dress reaches up above my white underwear and a sob rips from my lungs. I've had my thoughts, late at night, about someday lying down with a man, someone like Decker, somebody normal and gentle, probably fumbling. It never seemed like such a big deal, like something that would swamp me so completely with feeling. With humiliation and desire and the tug of linen up to the small of my back. The desk vibrates beneath me, the train vibrates beneath me, and I shake along with it, my body out of control.

Hades curses behind me, voice laden with something dark, edging on needy.

"You're a fucking liar. These clothes are all for

show, aren't they? You want people to believe you're as innocent as these panties say you are."

"I didn't think anyone would ever see them." I don't know what could possibly be a performance about what I'm doing now. If I'd had anything else to wear, I'd have worn that, but my mother threw out my school uniforms a long time ago.

"Except your boyfriend. You thought *he* might see them." He puts one finger under the elastic and traces a fiery path underneath, and then it's gone. "Did he like to play games with you, Persephone?" I've never heard a tone so deadly in my life. "Push you against a tree somewhere, let his hands creep up beneath your dress? Let other things beneath your dress?" One big hand caresses the back of my knee, then slips upward, upward, another inch, upward. And my own legs betray me. I'm completely frozen, hardly able to breathe, but at the touch of Hades' hand I move one thigh apart another inch. He laughs and I squeeze my eyes closed, which does nothing to keep the tears in. "You gave yourself to me all for the boy who taught you about getting pregnant?"

"No, he didn't," I finally manage. His fingertips play at the edge of my panties. He slips one underneath again, tugging it out, letting it snap back down. He's getting closer and closer to the softness between my legs and—and the dampness, and if he touches it, if he finds out, if he can see, I won't survive. There's no way I can live with the shame. But the moment comes anyway. Hades cups a hand over my panties, fitting it in between my widespread legs, and I can't stop the cry that he forces out. "Oh, god," I sob, rising up on tiptoe.

He goes still, but doesn't move his hand, waiting. One moment bleeds into the next.

"That's right," he murmurs. "Push back into my hand." My body obeys him, even if the rest of me wants to collapse to the floor. He fits his thumb into the cleft of my ass, and his fingertips—his fingertips brush a place only I've ever touched, and only secretly, only furtively, I would never have let Decker lift up my dress like this, not until we got married and moved into a house together. "You're fucking wet," he comments, a gravelly edge to his voice.

There's no arguing with him. I can feel it, too. And I can feel the tendrils of electric desire moving outward from that pressure. I grit my teeth. I will not move my hips to get him to make contact with my clit. I will not, I will not. But my hips betray me, too. It's hardly any movement, but it's there. I hate myself. I hate him.

"Who taught you to play this game, then?" He's searching for something, probing, and I don't know what. I never saw Decker inside the fence. We could never touch each other like this, even if I'd wanted to, and right now—I don't think I wanted him to touch me like this. *But you want Hades to touch you like this*, says that horrible voice. But I don't. I don't. "How many of the other farmboys did you fuck?"

As he says it, he works his fingers into the waistband of my panties, and the entire world grinds to a halt on its axis. There's only the vibration of the train beneath me, my hands somehow gripping the other side, and my toes trembling on the floor in my soft, ridiculous shoes. He's going to take the panties off and then he'll be able to see everything. He'll be able to *do* everything. He lowers the waistband, and the spiky edges of anticipation tear through me like a clawed beast. The words follow on a gasp, on a cry.

"I didn't fuck anyone." Tears, rain, there's no difference. "I'm a virgin."

Hades pulls the waistband away from my skin, hard enough that it digs in, then lets go. The hard snap against my skin brings me to my senses and restarts my lungs. I'm still wet between my legs, there's nothing I can do about that, but at least I still have the panties. That momentary relief doesn't last. My stomach turns over. Hades walks slowly around to the other side of the desk. I don't dare move until he reaches down and lifts my face from the wood, holding my chin in his hand.

"Don't fucking lie to me."

"I didn't—"

Something in his blue eyes chases the shakes away from my muscles, at least for now. I'm not fast enough for him. He reaches across and plucks me off the floor, knees barely clearing the surface of the desk, and plants me there in front of him in a little heap of linen. My legs are burning from standing on tiptoe and they sigh with relief—but as always, it doesn't last. He pulls me up to my knees. Wraps a hand around the back of my neck, tips me back. He's inches away, smelling like leather and cedar and something else, something that I've only ever smelled on him, looking into my eyes like he's seeing all of my thoughts skittering away from the surface of my brain. He's waiting, menace embodied, and every breath makes my breasts rise, aching for... something. His touch? Not likely.

"I said don't fucking lie to me," he growls. "Be a good girl and tell the truth."

Hades twines his fingers through my hair, tugging my head back another inch. *I'll do anything*. That's what I said. Telling the truth is part of *anything*.

"I was telling the truth before." I swallow and his eyes drop to the front of my throat, then come back up to meet mine. I sound hoarse, pained. "I'm a virgin. Nobody's ever—nobody's ever done that to me." My voice dries up in a whisper.

And Hades—Hades smiles, displaying a row of perfectly white teeth that have to be sharp enough to tear my skin. "But you've been waiting for it. Longing for it."

"No, I don't want it." I want it more than I can say. I want it enough to run away from home, I want it enough to leave my mother and everything I've ever known. But it's not just sex that I want. It's everything that comes along with it. Everything I *thought* came along with it. "I especially don't want it from *you*."

"Liar. You threw yourself at me. I've never seen a woman more desperate to be fucked."

Something breaks inside of me, crumbling under the tension and exhaustion from the night.

"You were going to kill him. I had to do something. I had to offer you *something*. And now—now..."

"Now you're going to get what you wanted."

A painful sob changes into a laugh in my mouth and I fall, tipping forward. I can't hold myself up anymore.

He catches me out of the air, saying nothing. I'm laughing too hard to do anything about it, swallowing the sound, putting my knuckles to my lips to keep it in. Better to let him think I'm crying. At least he likes that.

A door opens on a draft of air and a spike of panic drives deep into my brain. The bedroom, the bedroom. I land on the bed—a firm mattress, I've always wished for a firm mattress—and try to catch sight of him in the dim light coming in at an angle from the rest of the train car.

"What now? Is it time to pay more of my debt?"

But he only laughs. "You're so noble, Persephone. But I don't want noble from you."

"What do you want?" My lips are numb, useless, and in spite of myself my eyelids get heavier by the second. I reach for a pillow, tug it down under my cheek. Let him stop me. Let him do whatever he's going to do.

"Hmmm." He's above me, beside me, everywhere. "I want you to cry. I want you to beg. I want to watch your face go red with the shame you'll never be able to shake."

"I've done all that." My own voice sounds far away.

"You'll understand soon enough."

"I want—to understand now."

He leans close. "You'll beg because you want it."

I shake my head. "I won't."

"You will. Now go to sleep. I'm done with you for tonight."

8

HADES

GIVING in to every urge comes with a certain amount of pleasure, but nothing compares to denial. Denial of the body. Denial of the soul. Persephone is going to destroy what's left of my soul, I have no doubt. I thought there was nothing left, nowhere more depraved and empty to go, and yet here we are.

The train hurtles through the darkness. Persephone makes no move from the bed, and after a minute her breathing turns soft and even. She must know how defenseless she is, falling asleep here. She must also know that it doesn't matter. Persephone could have all the defenses in the world, and I'd still get to her. Everything is different now. Every fucking thing.

I hold out a hand to shake her awake, then decide against it.

There's no need to rush this, other than the insistent throb between my legs.

I made it clear I could kill her. She knows. She knows it down to her bones. But what *I* know is that I never will. Even if it would snap the tension winding through my ribs. Her heartbeat matters too much to me now.

If I break her now, reduce her to a little puddle of a woman, she'll be alive but not really living. I have the skills to do it. But I won't. I can't.

Denying myself her body is like wrapping my cock in barbed wire. I'm not fucking into that, but I can't resist drawing it out. She wants me to get on with it so badly. And I could. But I'd lose all those delicious tears, and the begging, and the way she fights so hard not to cry. If I break her now, all those tears will dry up. It would be such a pity.

I wipe my hands over my mouth, listening to her breathe. The darkness in here is far more tolerable than the lamp I left on outside. It almost seems plausible to lay down next to her and drift away.

Almost, but not quite.

I am more practiced in denial than most people I know, including and especially my brother. His lack of self-control is why tensions run so high in the city, all the different factions of people with their businesses, legal and illegal, jostling for his attention. He could never have kept himself from Persephone. I go back out into the main section of the car, turning that over in my mind. Surely he knows about Demeter's daughter. Surely he's seen her, or knows what she looks like. I have no explanation for his self-control when it comes to her. Perhaps he needs something from Demeter, too. My lips curl into a snarl. There's nothing I loathe more than needing something from someone else. I've devoted my life to exorcising every possible weakness, save the one I can't cut out.

I wave a hand over the light and it turns off, plunging the train car into darkness. Fuck, that feels good. I let myself sit heavily into the couch and press at my chest, trying to get that odd, painful sensation to go the hell away. It's not a heart attack, it's something deeper than that. Maybe an overabundance of lust. Or perhaps it's extra adrenaline, held back from when I almost killed that fucker but denied myself the pleasure. There is, if I'm honest in the privacy of my own mind, a layer in the depths that I don't care to acknowledge. It has shades of humanity. I hate it.

Should I turn the train around? I consider the question instead of assessing adrenaline-soaked emotions, tasting the sweetness of giving in to what I want, imagining every detail of what it would be like. The way the train would slow, the tracks rearranging themselves in front of us. Most people know there are provisions to change direction. Obviously, I would never fund a railway that could only go one way, inconveniencing myself to that extreme.

But it's too simple a taste for me, that sweetness. No, I won't turn the train around. I'll let myself want her while we go through the city and back into the dark, let it scratch at my skin, let my cock pulse against my pants.

I'll let myself suffer while she sleeps.

The communications unit pings on my desk. It's built to blend in with the surface and can even generate secure lines, if I ever needed it to. Its most convenient feature is its connection with my head of security, even when the train loses access to wifi.

"Answer," I tell it. Conor comes over and puts his head on my knee. I rub behind his ears, absently. He whines a little, tensing. "I'm fine. Settle down." He believes me for the moment. Conor has been with me since I moved out of the city. He's one of the only things I've ever been able to save from my brother Zeus—not that I place a high priority on saving anyone, or anything. It's almost always a pointless expenditure of valuable resources. But I hold a special well of hatred for Zeus in my heart. The fucker wouldn't know what to do with a good dog if it bit him, which a good dog would. I've tried not to become attached to Conor. He's only a dog, but he's good at what he does. He keeps me from wasting energy when it matters. And he has the virtue of being mine. He huffs, letting the weight of his head rest against me.

The call connects.

"Mr. Hades, Callahan here."

I hired Oliver Callahan almost directly out of the

streets, where he'd been living until the moment he decided to hitch a ride on the train and come raid the mountain. Never mind the insanity of attempting to perform petty theft in a fortress guarded by private security and by me—the motherfucker watched as the tracks split to send the train car into my private entrance, let himself get three electric shocks, and balanced on one of the connectors until he could get inside. I wasn't the one who gave him the long scar down his face, but if I had, he wouldn't have survived it. Somehow he managed to stay alive through that. Anyone with that kind of willpower is best kept loyal to me.

"Do you have an update?"

"No, sir. All the materials from Demeter's place were loaded without incident and the crew went home." All except one, of course. Conor lifts his head up and goes back in front of the fireplace. Curls up. Falls asleep.

"If you don't have an update, then why are you fucking calling me?" I lean my head back against the sofa and close my eyes. With a family like mine, there's a certain need for vigilance. The best part about the train is that it's exceedingly difficult to attack when it's going at full speed, and I know my men cleared the car before we started moving. This is one of the only places I can even pretend to relax. "If you killed someone again, there's no reason to give me all the details. Bury the body and move on."

He chuckles. "You didn't leave the platform for your meeting earlier. I wondered if you planned to turn back, or reschedule..."

Right. That needy, obnoxious ache in the center of my chest starts up again, and I sit up straight, rubbing at my eyes. The fucking moonlight. This was why I needed the meeting in the first place, but that's not going to happen now. Not now that I've got Demeter's daughter in my bedroom. That's certain to put a wrench in things. What difference does it make, in the end? Demeter was smart to hate me in the first place. Her paranoia keeps her safer than she would be otherwise, and to my great disgust and irritation I do need her to be safe.

"Callahan, if I wanted to turn back, I'd have given you the order already."

"Of course, sir."

"Don't call again."

The call disconnects with a two-toned beep, and I'm left alone in the train car. Wind whistles along the outside, a pleasant white noise. But the inside of my mind is rarely pleasant. The very moment the call ends she's back at the front of my mind, clinging to my shoulder and begging me not to kill that worthless sack of flesh. My cock reminds me of every angle—her delectable body bent over my desk, the way she had to spread her legs so wide to fit my hand, the way she fucking loved it.

I stifle a groan at how much she wants it—how much her body wants all the filthy things I'm going to do to her. And that admission she was a virgin—*fuck*. I knew she wasn't lying the first time she said it, but who doesn't like to push a little here and there? Make them spill a few more tears? Make them think it's their very last breath they're sucking in?

It's painful, how much I need to use her. I get up from the sofa in the dark and go over to the desk. Brace against it. Undo my pants with a swift jerk. Let her see me now. I'd love to see a brand-new wave of tears spill out of her eyes. Fuck, how she'd hate it if I made her come on my fingers, she'd hate it down to her bones, down to the center of her soul. Persephone has a soul, that much is obvious, and it's become my mission in life to dirty it up until she can't see any way to live without me.

I wait as long as I can, precum gathering on the tip of my cock, and then I take it in my fist and pump it hard, hips angled into the wastebasket, straining for the sound of her breath. I've taken her. I've bound her to me by her own words, a pretty extra on top of the fact that I was going to do it anyway. And yes, fucking *yes*, this will make things infinitely more complicated for me in the short term. There are certain things I need from Demeter in order to live my life. She can never know about Persephone. She finds out, it all comes tumbling down. But none of those complications do a thing to relieve the unfiltered lust rocketing through my blood.

The release is an anticlimax, empty and base, and as soon as it ends the cycle begins again. Sunrise, sunset. I lean against the desk and catch my breath. Fuck. Fuck. Taking her—that was easy. Making her cry, easier still. But keeping her at arms' length?

Curses fill my mind, and I fall back against the sofa.

Persephone believes I'll destroy her, and I fucking will—in every possible way that will still let me enjoy her. Only here, in the darkness of my train car, my cock already getting hard again, can I sit in the knowledge that this could be the end of me, too.

In far more ways than one.

9

PERSEPHONE

My eyes open on a darkness so complete a scream lurches up in my throat, and I clap my hands over my mouth, holding it back while I get my bearings. I can't see anything, and this makes the memories from last night even worse. Decker's slow kicks. The leisurely turn of Hades' head. His hand between my legs. I scrabble for something to hold onto and my hand meets a pillow.

A pillow. A bed. His bed.

My heart beats hard and sharp like I've been running. I made a deal, to save Decker's life, and I belong to Hades now. I tell it to myself again, and then a third time, but no amount of repetition makes it seem okay.

It is not okay.

It is not okay from every possible angle.

I press my knuckles against my eyes, wiping away the dried salt from last night. My skin is puffy and my face is probably still red. My hair—I don't have any way to fix the mess it's in. I smooth my hands over the curls and feel Hades' hand there too, the ghost of his touch from last night.

Last night or—or another night. How long has it been? How long did he let me sleep? He couldn't have actually told me to rest, could he have? A man like that wouldn't care about my beauty sleep. I fumble my hands together and whisper a half-remembered prayer that one of the girls in school used to say. I can't remember all the words, and I seriously doubt anyone will hear me. If last night taught me anything, it's that there is probably no God.

There is only Hades.

The door opens, sending me scrambling back on the bed, eyes stinging. The vibration of the train slows, then stops. I blink at the enormous figure in the door. Light streams in around him. I'm a mess, and he looks like he just stepped out of a walk-in closet. His jacket is back on. "Get up."

"What—where—"

"Sweetheart, I didn't say ask me questions about our location. I said, *get up.*"

I tip myself off the side of the bed. My shoes are missing—either I kicked them off in the night or Hades stole them, which seems unlikely. There's no time to look for them now. Not with him watching me. His eyes are hidden in the shadows but I can still feel where his gaze meets my skin. A strange heat. What happened before I slept taunts me. My cheeks must be the color of my mother's garnet-hued orchids. Or deeper. I open my mouth. Don't say anything. Shut it again. Don't. "But where are we?"

I have a small, wild hope that maybe we're in the city, and Luther Hades has decided to go back on our arrangement. He could let me off the train right now, even if he let me off alone, and I could proceed with the plan Decker came up with. Find somewhere to stay. Keep running. It's the smallest thing, like a newly hatched bird, and I know I'm being ridiculous by indulging it.

The slightest inhale of breath, which I recognize as a laugh.

"Where do you think we are?" He folds his arms over his chest, blocking more of the light. "Do you think I've brought you back home to run back into your mother's arms? Come here."

This time, I don't hesitate. Hesitation only ends with me crawling across the floor, and I don't want to cry again this soon after waking up. I stand one step away from him and he reaches down. With a rough grip he forces my face upward, fingers tight around my chin, so tight I almost gasp. He was playing with me last night. He was...he was being relatively gentle.

"You're. Never. Going. Home." Luther Hades doesn't bother to raise his voice. He lets the words cut me like the small knives that they are. "Not ever. Our agreement will never expire, not until you take your very last breath."

"Or until you take it from me." I shouldn't say it, I know I shouldn't say it, but it slips out on a wave of homesickness and regret.

A moment's pause, and then—

"That's right." His grip doesn't loosen but I think I heard a note of tenderness in his voice. Tenderness. Either that, or I'm still half-asleep. "Let's go."

He turns and walks away without looking back, and I want to throw myself into the darkest corner of the room and stay there until he forgets about me. Obviously, that's not an option—not with Conor stalking across the middle of the room. It's dangerous to be near Hades. It's more dangerous to be left in empty space near his dog. And I know he won't forget. He won't leave me behind. He made that clear last night. Very, very clear.

And as much as I hate him—and I do hate him, for what he did to Decker and for the fact that he's exactly as evil as my mother always said he was—there is a part of me that wants to see what happens next. A part of me that won't sit down and shut up now that I finally have a chance to do something other than roam my mother's fields. We're headed toward a logical conclusion, and god, that logical conclusion is terrifying. My heart thrums in my throat, just thinking of the waiting. But my mind recoils. *If he throws you down outside this train car and has his way with you, you'll be wishing you could go back in time to when it was all shrouded in mist, part of the future.*

I catch up as he steps down off the car, straining to hear Conor's footfalls behind me. The dog's nose brushes the back of my dress and my legs tense, ready to run. But running is the last thing you should do in front of a wild animal. He's *not* a wild animal, not really, but the back of my neck bristles like he is.

The platform outside is not just a platform. I get an impression of high ceilings and dark marble, a cavernous, echoing space. And then I get an impression of something else—something that needs a second look. Hades holds his hand out. The movement doesn't make any sense. What is he doing? What does he want me to do?

Oh.

He's offering me his hand. Conor bumps me to the side to get out, sending me into the doorframe.

Hades glares.

"Is it that you *want;* to fall onto the tracks? I can promise you, it wouldn't be a pleasant escape." His voice is so light and so cutting, all at once.

"No, I don't." I put my hand in his.

The touch is electric, bordering on a firestorm. For

all he touched me last night, the only thing I had under the palms of my hands were Hades' clothes. His hand is so big, and mine so small, like putting my hand into an alligator's cage. Utterly reckless and dangerous, if the alligator is in a bad mood. Hades is far more dangerous than any of the animals I've read about or seen outside the fence, except for his own dog. Is that what this is? A warning? Or my own body tricking me into thinking that a monster might not be so bad after all?

He tugs, and I step down. He doesn't seem to care that I'm not wearing shoes, or else he hasn't noticed. All around us, black-clothed men step into place in a loose circle. They've left enough space to make it seem like we're walking alone, but...we're not.

In fact, we're very far from alone. I've only ever seen the train station in the city, which was an antique design built before all the skyscrapers went up. At least that's what one of the placards on the wall said. This station doesn't have any placards. That doesn't seem to matter. It's busy. Nobody spares a second glance for his dog, which must mean they're used to it. I don't know how they could get used to a dog that size—one that's obviously a killing machine. I want to keep my eye on him, but the people demand my attention. So many people.

What did I expect, when he threw me over his shoulder? An empty room at the center of the mountain? This isn't it. Far overhead, the ceiling moves smoothly over us in a high arc. The rock is a matte black with streaks of gold painted onto it. No—not painted. In an instant, it clicks into place—he didn't hire artists to come hang from the rock, carefully imitating seams of precious metals. They are seams of precious metals. He's carved his train station out of his own riches.

"Close those lips, or I'll be forced to put something there," he says lightly, but I hear the promise in his tone.

"I—" What's the use in apologizing? There is none. I think—and I could be wrong—I think he likes it when I'm a little insolent. Probably because that'll give him an excuse to punish me later. A full-body shiver rocks me from head to toe. God, who has thoughts like this? Not me. I can't let myself sink into that kind of depravity no matter what happens to me here. If I do, I'll never be the same. And if I'm going to hold out any hope of escape, I have to keep myself intact. As much as I can manage. "This is huge."

People pour out onto the platform from doorways gashed into the walls. They keep their heads low. Their eyes flicker in our direction but the looks are glancing, temporary—these people head straight for the train, quick as they can. No wonder. I only wish I could ask them where they're going, and why it looks so simple for them to leave.

As if he's read my mind, Hades laughs. "They're not leaving, so wipe that precious expression off your face. They stay on the mountain, just like you will."

The trap of his hand closes over mine. "You keep people here?"

Hades looks at me like he's never seen a person quite as dense. "Who the hell do you think works in the mines, or staffs my home? Fucking commuters?"

"Just like me," I echo, the terrible realization dawning. "They all made a deal with you?"

His eyes narrow. "Did you think you were special?"

Maybe I did. Maybe some sound he made last night

made me think that his cruelty is hiding something else. But I must have imagined it. The way he's looking at me now, eyes harder than diamonds—no. I'm like everyone else in this station. I'm his property, too. My heart aches for them, and for me. I was desperate enough to throw myself on his mercy. They must've been, too. It's a cold comfort.

"You're nobody," he says simply, and even though I know it, even though I've been bracing myself all along, tears prick the corners of my eyes. "You're nobody now, and when I'm done with you, you'll still be nobody."

Then he lifts my hand to his lips and brushes them across my knuckles.

He drops it before I have a chance to react.

"Keep up with me. I don't have all day."

10

PERSEPHONE

THE MOUNTAIN IS MUCH FARTHER from my mother's fields than I thought. Nothing drives the point home harder than walking up the wide stone steps to a set of massive double doors that look like they've been carved from the same rock as the train station. They swing open as Hades and I approach, Conor right behind him, and it's only after a few seconds that I see the men holding them ajar. They both keep their eyes on the ground as we pass through and enter what can only be described as a capital city.

That's what it looks like, with Roman architecture and a soaring rotunda up at the top. A series of hallways branches out from the round center of the room. They're so long I can't see the ends from here. This palace isn't a mansion, this is a small city. Now it makes more sense why my mother would have been so paranoid—a man who could own something like this could own anything else he wanted, including the hands of an assassin or a policeman to look the other way. There are no rules for him—his house makes that crystal clear.

Something is not right about the space. Most places I've seen like this, in school and in pictures, are carved from...white rock, I guess. The rock shot through with gold isn't what's wrong about it, however. It's something else. Something is different. The shadows shift on Hades' face. I try to blink away the difference—maybe it's my eyes—but nothing changes.

People come and go here too, but fewer of them, and they're dressed in dark suits and maids' uniforms. All of them, without exception, subtly change their paths to get out of his way as we cross. I can't help craning my neck to look around as he moves through, not hurrying exactly but not giving me any time to look. There are carvings up in the dome of the rotunda, and windows. I can see white, fluffy clouds through the windows but the tint is off. Tinted windows in a rotunda? Who would ever want that? Lights ring the room, but the character of it doesn't measure up to natural light. It's not until this moment that I miss my mother's fields with a vengeance. I'd do anything for the sun on my face.

Hades stalks across the rotunda, footsteps echoing, to a bank of elevators. Conor keeps up, completely focused on following Hades. He doesn't pause to sniff the floor or get a pat from anyone else. He stays right by his feet like it's his job.

Maybe it is.

There's one button inset into a panel outside the elevator, and Hades presses it. The doors slide open soundlessly. Every set of doors reminds me of just how far I am from home, and safety. I don't want to go in, I don't, but I remember the way he bent me over his desk and I know he'd do worse right here and right now, no matter the audience. Maybe he'd like the audience. My core goes hot with embarrassment, and suddenly I can't get into the elevator fast enough. I break away and press myself against the back wall of the elevator, panting. My own reflection pants back at me. I have a moment to register that the flowers in my hair have...have died. Shriveled up, dried out into husks of themselves on my head. That should be impossible. They were new, from just yesterday.

But then Hades steps in. Conor follows. The doors close behind them. They're taking up all of the available space.

Hades narrows his eyes.

"What are you doing?"

It occurs to me that I'm gripping the handrail—I'm surprised there is a handrail in a place like this, where everyone is nobody—so tightly my knuckles have lost all their color. The elevator is far smaller than the train car, far closer, filled to the very top with my own fear.

"I'm being good. I'm staying out of the way."

"Being good." A smile plays over his face, beautiful and deadly. "What are you trying to avoid?"

Everything. "Getting bit by your dog."

He drops a hand to Conor's head. "If I wanted that to happen, it would have happened already. He's a very well-trained dog. He would never bite without my express permission. Anything else?"

"There's—there's nothing."

"You're not concerned about being punished?"

Maybe he wants me to let go, to stand closer, but I can't move. "You wouldn't punish me for trying to be good."

"My, my. I didn't think we'd come quite so far yet. Let's go back out so I can give you what you really want, you filthy thing."

"No, please." I hold on to the railing for dear life. "Don't do that, not now, not on the first day."

Hades saunters over. "So when you told me you would do anything to save your boyfriend, you meant *anything so long as you're nice to me*. You didn't really mean *anything*."

"I meant it." My heart has gone wild, uncontrollable.

"You'd submit to a punishment to prove it, then."

How could I do that? How could anyone do that? How could anyone just sit there and take it, no matter what they agreed? And why, *why*, does part of me already know the answer?

"Yes."

"You would *not*. Who are you trying to fool, Persephone?" His eyes have gone deeper than the center of me. They've gone all the way through. He can see *everything*.

"I have no other choice." My mouth has gone dry. "I would—I would try to do it."

"It's not about *trying*, it's about *submitting*." His hand is around my throat faster than lightning, too fast for me to raise my arms. "If you won't give me what you promised, then your word is useless. *You* are useless." He's not squeezing hard, not yet. Just enough to let me know he has absolute control. And my body—my body responds. My nipples tighten, and I press my ass against the wall of the elevator. Hades looks down into my eyes, watching my shame, and then he curses under his breath. "I can't fucking believe it." He almost sounds wondering. "Demeter's daughter is a virgin who wants a man to punish her."

I have never, *never* thought those words, even in the privacy of my own mind, even late at night when I know my mother is so soundly asleep that she'd never catch me thinking about it. But the truth—oh, god, the worst possible truth—is that I'm a liar. I'm a liar, and I have thought about a scenario like that, with a man's big hand and a woman bent over his knee, ass raised to—to accept it. There were books at school that I was forbidden to read, and I read them, but I never allowed myself to think of the words again. Only the images, and only because I knew it would never happen to me.

"No," I say, but it's weak. There's no fight behind it, and he sees that. That cruel smile spreads across his lips.

"You do." He dismisses me outright, and I want to slide down the wall of the elevator to the floor. "And to answer your question, though I don't believe you deserve an answer—I don't believe you deserve anything—is that you will lie down and take it whenever I see fit. You will do anything I demand of you. You'll take it because you have no choice."

At some point, the panting breaths have turned from panic to desire, which is terrible. It's the most terrible outcome I can imagine, aside from Hades dragging me back out into the center of the rotunda and punishing me. I don't even know what that would entail, other than—god, I can't even think about it. My body, however, has thought about it, and I can't deny the new dampness between my legs or the way my nipples brush against my tank top, sending electric shocks down to the center of my belly.

Hades studies me.

He studies me like I'm a foreign language to learn, and the only way to learn it is to absorb me into his skin until the humiliation eats me alive. Blessedly, that should happen soon. There's no way I can sustain that.

"Keep your hands on the railing."

I try to say *okay* but no sound comes out. Nothing comes out. I concentrate all my effort on the railing.

Hades kneels down in front of me, and even kneeling, he is absolutely in control.

"Punishment," he says, as if I've been a naughty schoolgirl, being intentionally obtuse, "can take many forms." He wraps two fingers around my ankle and lifts my foot off the ground, exposing the tender arch. "I could punish you here." He draws a finger down the center, the spot so sensitive I throw my head back against the wall and squeeze my eyes closed. Then the quick swipe of a fingertip on the tops of my feet. "Or here." God, what kind of horrible things does this man have up his sleeve? Is there no limit? *No*, whispers that voice. *There is no limit.* He drops my foot and runs two hands hard up the backs of my legs, then squeezes the backs of my thighs. "Here, until they're criss-crossed with stripes from my belt." His belt. Oh, my god, I might not survive this, not even one single day. His hands go upward, and he's testing the curve of my ass. "And here. This is what you were thinking of, I'm sure of it. A spanking. But you know, Persephone, there are far more interesting punishments."

I'm speechless, lips parted, struggling to take a breath. Heat, heat, heat between my legs, running up between my breasts. Hades thrusts his hands up to my chest, taking one breast in his hand. He studies it like he watched my face before, with complete concentration.

"Tits are an excellent thing to punish, too. The sounds—" He makes a noise of satisfaction. "Well, you'll see. But even more than that..."

There can't be more. There can't be more, because I'll die. I'll turn to dust in his hand and float away on the non-existent breeze in the elevator. He would love that, wouldn't he? Or would he hate it? I can't tell anymore, and the only thing that matters now in all the earth is the way he's touching me, roughly, squeezing, pinching. Why, why, why does it feel good? Why do I want to lift my hands from the railing, not to push him away but to pull him closer? What the hell is wrong with me? It's all so, so wrong.

Then he slips his hand down, over my tank top and over my panties—the same panties he palmed last night—and brushes his knuckles over a part of me that throbs in a desperate, aching way. He doesn't stay there. He reaches back behind me, takes two handfuls of my ass, and spreads. He's not even really touching me. That thin layer of fabric—that's keeping him from touching me. It's keeping his hands off my skin and it's not enough at the same time. It would be better if he took them off. But oh, god, it would be so mortifying, I would never be able to stand it, I would never live through that.

One of his fingers goes to a place so private I whimper, knocking my head back against the wall, anything to release the pressure. It only presses in harder, along with his finger.

"Here."

I'm babbling something, god knows what, the words meaningless. Hades pays no attention to them. He brings his hand around to the front of me and slots it between my legs, exactly where it was last night. He doesn't have to force them open. He's already arranged me how he wants me, and I didn't notice. He scrambles my brain. He does something to me that's worse, somehow, than killing me would have been. My mother was wrong, she was wrong.

"And here."

All the sound and breath in the elevator goes still. Letting go of the railing isn't an option—it hasn't been on the table since he told me to keep my hands here—but he might as well be holding me up with his hand between my legs. It's awful, it's wonderful, and it's going to tear me to pieces. Seconds tick by in the silence. He's waiting for something. I pick my head up from the wall and look down at him, my face burning.

"You—you wouldn't. You wouldn't do that."

He looks up at me, serious expression on his face. I think of a judge handing down a sentence, paternal in a way and vaguely concerned. I've taken you through this as simply as possible, the look says. Are you still not following?

"I would. Know it in your heart, Persephone. I would."

Hades stands up, brushing his hands together like he's done dirty work. The moment snaps apart. I bend forward, bare feet hot and then cold on the elevator floor. He turns, eyes already far away, and presses one palm to a panel on the wall that glows. The elevator drops, my stomach rises, and we descend into what has to be Hades' private rooms.

11

PERSEPHONE

THE ELEVATOR COMES to a smooth stop and the doors slide open. I swallow back a bitter surge of fear. The way time passes is distorted by standing so close to Hades, so I have no idea how long we've been dropping down. We could be far below the mountain, for all I know. Outside the doors the hallway drops into shadow. Is it a dungeon? Is he going to lock me up in a cage? That empty train car comes back to me in full force. He would do that. He'd shut me behind a solid rock door with nothing but my clothes and keep me there, the weight of the mountain crushing me bit by bit until there's nothing left.

He steps out into the hall. Conor moves first, going directly to his side. Hades looks back. His face in profile, even wearing an expression of impatience, is so beautiful it takes my breath away.

"Let go of the fucking railing. Don't be tedious about this. It wastes my time."

I'm trying to be good, I want to say, but I don't. It disgusts me, trying to be good. Who have I become? Less than a day away from home, and I'm already scrambling and scraping to please him. I have to stop. I can't stop. I can never, ever stop.

I follow him out and try to keep myself calm by going over the details. This is not, at first glance, a dungeon, like I've read about in my books. Dungeons don't have walls carved like this, with the same gold streaks I saw below. This floor—this wing?—has no echoing rotunda. The ceilings are high enough that Hades looks almost normal. This place was made for him, as custom as his suits. I steal a glance behind us. The hall disappears into darkness in either direction.

He sighs.

I snap my head around, expecting to see him glaring at me, but he's standing with his eyes closed, hands in his pockets. It lasts for less than a heart-beat. Conor nudges him below the knees, almost like he's coaxing him to go somewhere. As if Hades could ever be coaxed. Hades opens his eyes, frowns at me, and moves down the hall, Conor at his feet. I'm not even as good as his dog.

"Keep up."

What was that I saw? Relief at coming home? Hades is a man who should be as comfortable here as he is anywhere else. There's nothing that could possibly touch him, out there in the world or here at home. Does he...like being at home? Need it, like regular people do? It doesn't seem possible, and yet...

We pass four doorways and the gloom lifts at the end of the hall, where a double door is set into the end. We're almost there when I can't force my feet to go another step. Hades stops and looks around to me, scowling now.

"I said, keep up."

"Just tell me what's going to happen," I plead.

He rolls his eyes. "When I said I'd make you beg, I didn't mean over every obnoxious thought that goes through your mind. I thought that was understood."

Anticipation and anxiety twist together at the center of my chest, filling up all the space where air is supposed to be.

"I can't stand it," I say breathlessly. "I need to know what's coming. I need it."

Hades makes his way back over to me, a half-smile on his face. Oh, he understands, he understands. My heart cracks open with relief. I know he's a bad man. I know he doesn't care about me and never will. That doesn't mean he's incapable of all empathy. He must see in my face how much I need this. Is it a dungeon? A cell? Did I make a mistake, thinking this was his home, and not a prison? Why would I think the walls would matter? Why, why, why? My thoughts become more and more tangled with every step he takes.

He reaches out and puts a hand on the top of my head and I let my eyes flutter closed. A comforting touch. I thought I'd never feel a comforting touch again. One tear, then two, comes free of my eyelids.

His thumb rubs over my temple, smoothing back my hair. I need this. I need this so much. I press my lips together to keep my chin from quivering, because I don't want him to stop, I don't want—

Hades digs his hand into the back of my hair, twists his fingers in hand, and tilts my face up to his. It pulls a gasp from my mouth. I've never seen a harder, more narrowed set to his eyes, not even when he was killing Decker.

"We're not going to do this." Nothing about him is loud, which makes his voice sound far deadlier. This is a man who doesn't even have to speak to keep people in line. "I'm not going to pet you and indulge you at every single fucking doorway. You need to know what happens? You already know what's going to happen, sweetheart. You'll do anything I say and maybe, *maybe*, I'll let you live. But let's get down to the truth at the very bottom of this, the one you keep flirting with and trying to get me to deny. If I want you to die, you'll die. You belong to me now."

I stare, open-mouthed, caught halfway between abject terror and disbelief at how beautiful he can look when he's being so mean.

Hades gives my hair a shake and I cry out a little at the pain.

"Do you understand me?"

"Yes," I choke out.

"That's not good enough, sweetheart. Tell me what it is you understand."

"That I—" I suck in a deep breath, hoping it'll give me enough momentum to get the words out. "I belong to you now."

"Again." He pulls my hair, harder, tipping my head back. Hades leans his head down until his lips are an inch away from my skin. He could bite me now, break the skin, and let me bleed out on the floor. All I feel is his hot breath as he exhales. "I said *again*. How many times do we need to go over this? Or is it that you're really begging for punishment? I promise you, Persephone, I can make it so you'll never, never forget what I've told you."

"I belong to you now." This time, my voice is low and frantic.

"I can't hear you."

"I belong to you now!" His hand digs in and the pain my scalp blooms into something sharper, all-encompassing. "I belong to you now! I belong to you now! I belong to you now, please, I belong to you now," I scream the words, sob them, he's going to pull me backward, he's going to let me hit the floor. Instead he pulls my hair upright, toward the ceiling, and lets me fall.

My knees hit the floor with a bruising blow and I put my hands to the back of my head, expecting to feel blood. A hand comes down to my chin, pulling me up to my feet. I can't catch my breath, but somehow, that hand steadies me. Something else does, too—Conor, pushing against me. Almost like he's pushing me up. The dog makes a low noise in the back of his throat, and for the life of me, I can't tell if it's comforting me or trying to get me back on my feet to do Hades' bidding. He presses his nose against the crook of my arm, the rest of him warm and solid. Everything is upside down. I should not feel any safer here, with Conor at my side. But I do.

Hades eyes trace my face, following my tears down to my chin.

"Excellent," he murmurs. "You have no idea how much I fucking loved that."

"You're sick." I shouldn't say it, not if I want to keep breathing, but the lingering pain overrides what's left of my good judgment. "Disgusting. Vile—"

"That's it," he prompts.

"You're a terrible man," I shout.

"Well, yes."

"You're the worst person I've ever met." The last tears fall, then dry on my cheeks. The air here—it's not still, or stuffy, despite the lack of windows. It's always moving, always whispering against my skin. "I hate you."

"Good." Hades pats my head again, a light in his eyes, a smile playing around his lips. What the hell? "I intend to strip you down to the very core of you, Persephone, and make you mine in ways..." He trails off with a chuckle. "But this bullshit of yours, these little fits of terror over things like doors...save it."

"Save it?" I cross my arms over my chest to hide the shake in my hands. "Save it for what? This is all—this is all very, very bad." My throat begins to tighten with tears so I clear it roughly.

"Save your pretty fear for when I have you naked over my knee or tied spread-eagle on my bed." He swipes his thumb across the remnants of my tears, the salt-tracks that seem to be a constant fixture on my face now. "That's when I want it. Don't waste it on things like entering a room. You'll exhaust yourself, and that will limit the amount I can enjoy you. That's not what I want. Say it one more time, so I'm absolutely sure you understand."

His words echo in my brain—naked over my knee, spread-eagle on my bed—and I imagine stuffing them into a closet and shutting the door. It's the only way I can make myself say it. Because I don't belong to him. I'll never belong to him, not truly.

"I belong to you now," I repeat, voice level.

"That's right." He whistles. "Conor, go in."

The door swings open beneath his hand like it was waiting for him to open it, and Hades sweeps one hand around my back and pushes me into the room. The dog shoots past us and disappears down one hallway. One of my bare toes catches on the smooth floor and I stumble, but this time there's nobody to catch me. He's behind me, and there's no way for anyone to—

A hand flies out in front of me just as I catch my balance and I take it like it's the last life preserver on a sinking ship.

"Thank you. Thank you so much..." The gratitude

dies on my lips as I straighten up, the new information falling into place.

Someone reached out to catch me.

Someone has been inside this room the whole time, hearing what happened, hearing me scream.

I raise my red, hot face only because I can't stand the wait any longer.

Five women in black uniforms, their hair combed back in sleek buns, wait in a semicircle in the entryway to the most enormous room—it must actually be a set of rooms, because this is no bedroom. To call it a living room seems like a ridiculous understatement. Thick pillars separate an enormous sunken sitting area from the rest of the room. It looks ancient and modern at the same time—like you could curl up at the base of it and stare into a screen or sit around the edges and attend a performance. My heart zigzags frantically at the thought of what kind of performance that would be. Knowing what I know of Hades, it could be...

The blood leaches out of my cheeks and I take a step back toward Hades. He nudges me forward again with a sharp exhale. I've annoyed him again.

One of the women—the one who put out her hand to break my fall—looks to be in her forties, with silver hair and a red lipstick that makes me feel utterly naked in its perfection. I look ridiculous, here in this room. A linen dress, handmade for me by an old lady my mother pays by the season? I want it off. If I could have anything else to wear, I'd wear it.

"Fix her," says Hades. "Don't disturb me until it's done."

He moves past me as the women close in, the lady nearest me reaching for my hand again. Hades doesn't look back. He heads to a wide hallway leading god knows where.

"You're leaving?" I call after him.

"What does it look like?"

"I thought you would stay." I try and fail to keep the quiver out of my voice.

"They're in charge now," he says lightly, still not turning back, still not bothering to see if I'm all right. He doesn't care, he doesn't care, of course he doesn't care. "Obey their orders as if they've come from me."

"I'm Genie," says the lady with the silver hair. She doesn't bother to look where he's gone. Her eyes hold a flicker of concern, then her face settles into seriousness. "Come this way, Persephone. We can't keep Mr. Hades waiting."

12

HADES

Persephone would collapse into a fit of tears if she knew about the two-way mirror.

It's made with slightly different technology than the rest of my windows, which means the wall doesn't even appear to have a window in it. There are many reasons for me to have a room in my private quarters that allows for observation, but of all of them, this is by far the most enjoyable.

I sit on a sofa designed to my exact specifications, to fit someone of exactly my height and stature, and watch through the window as Genie and her team do their work. There have been other women in Persephone's exact position before. That's why the rest of them are here, waiting to do my bidding. I tend to keep people around once they've proved their usefulness. I chuckle to myself at the joke. Almost everyone here, aside from a select few, is here because they owe me their lives.

Make a decision, pay the consequences. It's simple. Persephone acts like she has no experience with consequences, but I can't imagine that's true. Demeter has never been the kind of woman to live and let live. It explains everything, from the farm-girl dress to the way Persephone blanches at the sight of an unfamiliar door. She's been kept quarantined all her life.

Which makes her the perfect thing to be mine.

To *make* mine. She is a blank slate, waiting to be shaped.

This will have an effect, no doubt. Through the window, I watch as Genie strips off Persephone's dress, leaving her shivering and clutching her arms to her chest.

"Oh, please. It's not as if it's cold."

She doesn't answer, obviously. I focus instead on her

pink cheeks and the nipples poking out underneath her tank top. What the hell is that thing? What the hell was Demeter's plan, to keep her virginal and dress her in nightgowns for the rest of her life? She couldn't have run away to the city in those clothes. Ah—of course. Demeter didn't just want to keep her safe, she wanted to keep her incapable. Well, she very nearly succeeded.

Genie demands the tank top next, and Persephone reddens, shaking her head. I could turn the sound up and hear the audio from the next room crystal-clear, but this silent-film shit is better. It forces me to pay closer attention to her body when I'm not distracted by the sound of her voice.

Good woman, that Genie. She only lets Persephone argue with her for a very short time before she calls the other women. I assume she's threatened to hold her down and cut the clothes off, because Persephone strips in a hurry.

I can't tell if this display of humiliation is quite real or if Persephone is playing some other game. She stares down at her feet, hands clutched in front of that sweet little pussy of hers, her cheeks a blazing red. But I felt how wet she got yesterday in the train, and again on the elevator. I saw how much she wanted me to fuck her.

Perhaps she gets off on the humiliation. She wouldn't be the first in the world. But she would be the first to hold my attention like this. On a few occasions,I've directed Genie to teach the woman a short lesson. Now, I'm struggling to let anyone else touch her.

My phone rings, interrupting my view of the first bucket of water hitting Persephone's naked skin. I catch a glimpse of her gasp and the way she raises her hands to her eyes to wipe the droplets away, and pull the damn thing out of my pocket.

It's my brother.

The fucker.

"What do you want?"

"That's some way to say hello, Luther." Zeus sounds mildly disapproving, as if he has any fucking right to have the slightest opinion on how I answer the phone. "I'd think you'd have a more pleasant greeting for your brother."

"I'm busy."

"So that's a no, then."

"It's a no to you, asshole. If you're calling me just to be irritating, then hang up the phone now and spare us both the breath."

The women in the next room have coordinated forces to scrub Persephone clean, standing there in the middle of the room. I can't see the drain from here but I know they've arranged her over it. They lift one of her arms above her head, which has the delightful effect of lifting her tits along with it. Then the other arm. Hands on every part of her, none of them mine. I grit my teeth. Genie points to her feet, then points again, and with an expression of agony Persephone parts her legs so they can wash her there, too. I would do this myself—fuck, I want to—but I don't want to give her the impression this early on that I care for her in any way.

Even if I do.

"—very rude," Zeus is saying. "It's obvious you're not listening."

"It's obvious you didn't have a reason to call." I shift positions on the sofa. "Here's some politeness for you. Goodbye."

"Don't hang up, Luther."

"Why the hell not? Does it ever occur to you that I might be preoccupied? I don't sit around waiting by the phone like one of your...conquests." I almost called them whores, but the women who are attracted to Zeus aren't anything of the sort. If I cared, I might call them victims. But I don't care. I gave up caring a long time ago.

"Of course you're busy." He sighs. "You're always busy. Too busy to participate in the family..."

I snort a laugh. "Stop fucking with me, you monstrous waste of time and flesh."

"You wound me."

"You make me ill." This is not just an offhand remark. I'm at least giving Zeus the courtesy of the truth. For all I've been...rough...with Persephone, there's something different about my situation with her. For one thing, I have to keep her safe. Something happened when I brought her onto the train. Something I don't want to admit out loud, and perhaps I never will. She's a liability now, and it's made all the more complicated by the fact that I can't kill her. We've never met before, but I have the ridiculous sensation that I've known her all her life. Or perhaps it's that her life has just begun.

She's a danger to me, and I can't kill her. I fucking won't.

If only I could kill my brother without causing the family business to collapse.

But that's neither here nor there.

"I'll wait if you need to be sick," Zeus says, almost tenderly.

"Goodbye."

"Tell me, Luther." Now he speaks quickly. I hate Zeus with every fiber of my being, but even hating him with this intensity can't erase our childhood together. He knows when I'm going to follow through. "Did you take her?"

My heart slows, almost to a stop. Through the window Persephone is doused with another bucketful of water. One of the women is filling them again and again. They turn her so I can see her wet curls falling down her back. That. Fucking. Ass. I want her bent over my desk again. Need it.

Genie moves around behind Persephone and starts to work something out of her hair. Flower petals, dried up and dead. I killed them myself, the day that I finished this house.

"Damn it, Hades, listen to me."

"Fuck right off," I tell him genially, even though my heart has gone frozen and still. Someone in my staff is going to die for this. Someone must have seen us get off the train and leaked the news to Zeus somehow. This place is crawling with rats.

Or...is it, really? My livelihood depends on making deals with people who desperately need them, or at least people who desperately need me to not kill them. Is it fair? No. But the need to live doesn't decrease for them. And I have them watched, of course I do. I'd know if there was a mole here. A traitor.

"This is a serious question."

"No it's not." I let him hear every moment of my long-suffering sigh. "You haven't even told me who you're talking about. If it were that urgent, you'd have gotten straight to the point."

"Demeter's daughter is missing."

"Oh? What a terrible pity. The little slut probably ran off to the city. Like mother, like daughter." My pulse presses out against my veins, the blood too big for the space it occupies. It's an obnoxious distraction from both things I'm trying to focus on. Like Genie leading Persephone over to a waxing table, and her eyes getting wider and wider as Genie explains what she's going to do. I get to my feet and pace over to the window, swallowing hard. Half of me wants to run in there and throw all their hands away from her. *Mine*, I would growl, loud enough to scare the shit out of them. The other half is relishing her embarrassment and fear, even from here, and certain of one thing—she'll know better than to trust the people who work for me.

I am also listening to Zeus. I can almost hear his pathetic mind trying to decide if I'm only dodging the question or if I really have nothing to do with this. The moment lingers, expands. I'm going to die of a fucking heart attack, and that will be a great loss to everyone who still owes me. Zeus sure as hell won't make their lives any better. They might think he will. They'd be wrong.

Genie is a professional, but Persephone shakes so badly she has to call the other women to hold her down. To spread her open so she has the access she needs. Genie must guess that there's a window, because I catch the flicker of her glance in my direction. She must know that I watch her to ensure that the job is done correctly.

To ensure that it takes perhaps longer than necessary.

Persephone's chest rises and falls, quickly, quickly, tears leaking down her cheeks. Genie applies the wax, the strip, and waits.

A heartbeat. Another heartbeat. She says something to Persephone, then rips it away.

Persephone arches back on the table, biting down on her lip. It takes all of them to keep her in place. She lifts her head, and I can tell by the wide-eyed look in her eyes that she's begging.

But Genie is a good employee. She knows better than to cross me. *We have to keep going,* her lips say, silent.

Persephone squeezes her eyes closed.

More wax. Another strip.

I am desperate, fucking *desperate*, to go into the room right now and shove my fingers inside of her. She'd be soaked, no question. Those red cheeks, those nipples—everything about her gives her most private thoughts away, as if she'd said them out loud.

The third strip.

She turns her head into the palm of one of the women holding her down and weeps.

But she doesn't close her legs.

Fuck.

The scene draws all the blood down from my brain and into my cock, splitting my concentration in a very unpleasant way. I have to turn away from the window to finish the conversation. Conor stirs on the low bed in the corner and lets out the beginning of a whine. He thinks something's going on—that I have to get out of here. I do, but not for the reason Conor thinks. I signal him back to his rest. I'm still fucking fine. Mostly.

"I'm far too busy to stand here listening to you breathe in my ear, Zeus."

"She's very upset," he says, voice sounding far away.

What I can't figure out is why he cares. Zeus doesn't care about anyone. That's the core of his personality. That is why he has bastard children all over the city and even a couple of settlement agreements with women who had nothing to lose when they went after him. I'm sure he's only biding his time when it comes to them, too. People flock to that man because they confuse beauty with trustworthiness. A smile with a kind heart. He slips those disguises on and off like a comfortable jacket, whenever and wherever it suits him. They can call me what they want—a killer, a monster, a sadist—but no one can ever say I hid it from them.

"It's not my concern if she's upset because her brat ran away." Concern—who cares about concern? The only thing that matters to me is the deal I've made with Demeter. And she'd never go back on that, because she can't. I don't renegotiate.

That—and Persephone.

A prickle of unease wakes in the back of my mind. Demeter wouldn't go back on our agreement. Would she? Demeter's daughter is no longer a child. She can't possibly have expected to keep her locked away in her home until she dies. And anyway, it's too late now. I have her here. Unfortunately, turning away from the window has only made it harder to think. Imagining what's going on a few feet behind me makes my heart pound. I turn my head and steal a glance. Genie has Persephone in the most humiliating position I could have imagined on the waxing table, and her face is such a delightful red color that I wish I could capture it in a painting. Her lips form one word, over and over. *Please, please, please.*

"What the fuck was that noise?" Zeus sounds disgusted. "Are you fucking someone?"

"You're the only one rude enough to take phone calls when you're using a woman," I shoot back. But something else is happening behind my breastbone, something very unexpected. Lying about Persephone feels like a cousin to protecting her. Protecting her, as if she meant anything to me. The thought of her name on Zeus' lips makes me want to drive my fist through his face, and he hasn't even said it yet. I lean hard on the sill of the two-way mirror. I can't take my eyes off her. A screeching alarm sounds in the heavy silence of my thoughts. *A weakness*, it cries. *She is your weakness.*

Fuck.

He sighs, irritated. "If you come by any information, you'll tell me?"

I give him a pause to make him think I'm considering it. "Fuck no," I spit into the phone. He's still trying to talk to me when I stab my thumb down onto the button to cut off our connection. It falls to the floor with a loud clatter. I crush it under the heel of my shoe, again and again and again, until the plastic casing splinters and the wires inside come apart. What have I done, and what am I doing? What does this instinctive lying say about me now? In the end I sweep the shattered phone into one corner with the toe of my shoe, rage hardly spent.

Yes. Fine. I've created a small problem, a dangling thread that will irritate me until I cut it off at the neck. What the fuck do I do about Demeter? The question pales in comparison to the issue of Persephone. Because I can't live without Demeter and what I buy from her.

And I can't live without Persephone.

It's an absurd thing to admit, even in the privacy of my own mind. It doesn't suit me to feel this way about anyone or anything, even in some dim, vague way that disappears as soon as I look at it head-on.

On the other side of the window, Persephone sits up on the table, breasts heaving with every breath. And as I watch, she turns toward Genie, my name on her lips.

13

PERSEPHONE

GENIE SLIPS a dress that's more of a slip, a night-gown, over my head, eyes sharp and lips pursed. She reaches down and tugs the hem into place. It barely covers my ass. It was made to barely cover my ass. I don't bother asking if there's a bra and panties to go with the set. Clearly, there's not, and clearly, her orders came from Hades himself.

"Good." She gives the rest of her team a crisp nod. "I'll be back in a few minutes to assist with cleanup." Genie flips over her wrist and her eyes widen at the time. "If you'll come this way..."

I follow her without a word, because what's the point? I'm officially nothing. My own embarrass-ment has burned me so many times that it's surprising to discover, at every new moment, that I'm not just a pile of ashes. Sweep me up with a broom and set me free on the wind. But again, and again, every heartbeat reminds me that I'm still here. In this body that's been waxed and stripped and buffed until I'm not sure I have my original skin left. They put lotion on my stinging flesh, every inch of it, and worked out all the tangles from my hair. I've never been so sensitive and so numb in all my life.

"This way," Genie says, tone urgent. I pick up the pace. I've been staring at the floor, under the polished marble beneath my feet.

"Where are we going?" The question comes more out of resignation than anything else. I don't expect her to answer. I think of Hades' fingers in my hair, and how Genie probably heard me screaming, and didn't do anything about it. Nobody will ever do anything about it again.

And how maybe, *maybe*—

No. I can't let myself think that way, otherwise all my sacrifice will have been for nothing. It's not a sacrifice if some twisted part of your soul enjoys it. And I don't. I can't. He's evil, and he's done so many horrible things already. I'm...I'm in shock, that's all. It's been a shocking turn of events. It's not my fault if that makeover session made me think of him. I hated him then, too. I hate him now, and I love Decker. I say a silent prayer for Decker, *to* Decker, and let the memory of him standing in the fields carry me through one breath, then another.

"To meet with Mr. Hades." Genie's voice breaks into my memory.

"To...meet with him?"

"He wanted me to prepare you for a meeting with him."

I laugh, the sound surprisingly...real. Genie raises her eyebrows and picks up the pace.

"Is that what he calls it? He's a very proper man."

"He likes things to be a certain way." Her silver hair bobs behind her in its bun.

The hallways of Hades house are proof of this. Every one of them gleams with a kind of blank perfection that makes the weird quality of the light seem less unsettling. That can't possibly be for other people, so there is a man underneath that cruel facade that has feelings one way or the other. There must be. Genie takes me this way and that until I've lost all sense of where that prep room was, and then, abruptly, she makes a sharp right turn off the hallway, almost colliding with a woman in a black dress and white apron—one of the maids.

"I'm on my way in," says Genie in a low voice. "Anything I can take for you?"

The maid nods, lips pressed into a serious line. "This." She hands Genie a small silver tray with a phone, shiny and slick, in the center. "Thank you."

Genie waits until the maid has scurried off down the hall to push open the door with one elbow.

It's an office.

Hades' office.

Genie goes directly to his desk and puts the tray down on the far corner, getting out of the way as fast as she can.

Hades sits behind an enormous desk, Conor off to one side, head bent over a stack of papers. The office...it's too normal for him, all dark wood paneling and low lights. I feel like I'm seeing him stripped down to nothing in a room like this. The rotunda in the entryway of this...fortress is meant to impress people, but this looks like a truly private room.

"Mr. Hades." Genie glances around for me, then gestures me forward, into the pool of light surrounding his desk.

Hades looks up from his papers.

His eyes land on me like ice water, cold and assessing, and an answering heat sears through my lungs, down to my belly. My body doesn't know how to react to him. My stomach twists, then relaxes. How can I be glad to see him? How can any part of me be glad to see him? His eyes travel slowly from the top of my head down to my still-bare toes, and when they meet mine again, the frigid stare has slipped away. It's darker now. Hotter. The hairs on my arms stand on end.

"Go now."

Genie nods and leaves, shutting the door behind her with a soft click that is the loudest sound on the planet.

I'm alone with him now. Heart hammering. Legs trembling. For all I've gone through, he still makes me shake and shiver. The skimpy dress isn't helping.

All the possible things he could do rush through my mind. Will the dress survive? Will *I* survive?

No matter how many times I tell myself it doesn't matter, it still does.

Hades seems to take up every spare inch of the room. There isn't a single breath that's not suffused with him. And he smells...clean. Like leather and cinnamon and a lungful of cold air. I resist the urge to fold my hands over my chest. It won't hide anything from him. It'll only make him notice me more, and now that Genie's done with me, there's more to...notice.

A blush creeps across my cheeks.

"Stop staring and sit down."

There's more than one chair in his office, and that familiar panic crawls up the back of my spine and shakes the base of my neck. Move. He must mean the chair in front of his desk. Easy enough. Breathe. While I pad forward and take a seat, he lifts the phone from the tray and flicks it on, then puts it down on the edge of the desk closest to him.

He watches me for far longer than is necessary. He must be able to see me from where he sits, with the wide desk separating us and nothing else. I bite my lip. It's strange that he's not bending me over it, fisting his hand in my hair. Isn't it? Or are things different in his fortress?

Hades curses low under his breath, narrowing his eyes. "Fuck. I can smell you from here."

My stomach sinks and I curve forward, wanting to disappear underneath the desk, underneath the floor, and underneath the earth itself.

"I didn't—I don't—"

He leans forward. "It's making it difficult to proceed with our task. Don't hunch over like that, Persephone. It doesn't suit you. If I want you humiliated, I'll do a better job than that, I assure you." A shake of his head, like he's clearing his thoughts. "With a pussy like that, you'd think someone would have laid claim to you already. Not that I care about other people's claims." This last bit is soft, almost like he's talking to himself. "It does explain why your mother kept you behind lock and key."

"She wanted to protect me." We cannot be talking about this. My face will superheat and I'll never recover. The question hovers at the tip of my tongue, but I don't dare ask what the task is. "She thought that men might want to hurt me."

"I won't hurt you." A fleeting grin. "Very badly, at any rate."

He will. He *will.* He already has. But it could get worse. That's what he means, isn't it?

"You don't mean that."

"I do. I won't hurt you enough to kill you." Hades glares at me from across the expanse of wood. "How much time are you planning to spend on these ridiculous questions?"

He sounds...different. Like something happened between when he handed me off to Genie and now. A mask. It reminds me of slipping on a mask.

"What's our task?"

"Finally." He pushes the stack of papers across to me, and I try to get control of my breath and my mind. "It's time to formalize the terms of our agreement."

"Formalize them?"

"With a written contract, yes."

None of this makes any sense. He already has me here. He's already...made me over to his specifications. He's made it so clear that I'll never leave. What difference could it make for me to sign a paper?

"But why?"

The corner of his mouth rises, and he shakes his head. "What kind of operation do you think I've built, sweetheart? One that runs on a person's honor? Hardly. Everyone signs their name to their promises here."

It's the hardest thing I've ever done, scanning the words on the papers. They all blur together, the letters switching places and taunting me. But there it is, in black and white. Decker's name. My name. The offer I made. In the contract, he's written submission without limits. I think of my terrified *I'll do anything* and wonder how he could have described it like that. *Submission without limits.* I bite my lip and read it again, then again. It doesn't sound like something I should want, on any level.

And yet.

If I signed this paper, I would never have to question what my life would be again. There would be no more making plans to get away. No more wondering if Decker could really hack life in the city or if I'd end up running back to my mother. No more worrying about running into dangerous men on the street. The most dangerous man would be here, right where I could see him at all times.

I crave it—that relief. My hands tremble around the paper. I'm not supposed to be this way. And I didn't come here because I wanted someone to tell me what to do, I didn't. I wanted to stop being told what to do. I wanted to be free, and now...

Now I don't know what I want, with my skin still humming from all the contact and every part of me leaning closer in to get another breath of him. It doesn't make sense. I want to scream.

But I swallow that scream and try again to order my thoughts.

"What happens if I don't sign?"

A brief fantasy touches down like a lightning strike—a ride on the train, and then slipping back into my bedroom in time to pretend I'd only wandered out into the fields for the night. That I'd momentarily found myself wishing for air and space, so I went out and slept under the trees.

My mother would never buy it.

And Decker...

"You exchanged your life and submission for that useless fuck's life," Hades says simply. "If you decide not to keep your word, then I won't keep mine."

My heart stops, then starts again.

"Then—" Every thought is like a statue carved from stone. It takes forever for the shapes to be revealed. "Then he's still alive?"

Hades shrugs. "I can't be sure."

"You don't know what happened to him last night?"

"I told my people to take him where all trespassers go." Hades sounds impatient, like I should have known all this in advance. Like someone should have taught me. "To work in the diamond mines until they're no longer of use to me."

I swallow a bitter fear. "So you'll kill him eventually anyway."

He flicks his eyes toward the ceiling. "The better question is, why do you care? Why would you want to run off with a man who blunders into situations with people like me? He'd last five minutes in the city. Maybe less, with you hanging off his arm." Hades grins at me. "He's lucky, in a way. I didn't take you from him on a busy street corner. Very few people got to see him be so thoroughly put in his place."

"So I have to sign this. And if I don't sign, you'll kill Decker, and you'll kill me too."

His mouth tightens. "I doubt I'd bother. If you don't sign, I'll release you."

"What?" Shock tunnels through me, twisting itself up with confusion. And, somehow, disappointment. A sick, wrong disappointment. I shouldn't want this man to touch me, not ever again. "You'll take me home?"

"I'll *release* you," he says slowly, drawing out every word. "If you can make it down the mountain and follow the tracks back to your mother's house, then I suppose you could go back there. But no one here will give you a lift." Hades rubs a hand over his mouth. "In all likelihood, you'll just die alone in the wilderness, wearing...exactly what you're wearing right now."

I read the papers again.

Hades taps his fingers on the desk. "I don't offer renegotiation of this sort as a matter of course, Persephone. Don't make me wait. If you're going to take advantage of it, do it now."

I feel...small. Unworthy of understanding this contract in my hand. It has clauses guaranteeing that I'll be fed and clothed. It says he can discipline me at will. The more I read, the more I want to cry. Only I don't know if I'm crying because there's no way out of this or because I don't want a way out of this. It doesn't bother me as much as it should, his control over my body. It bothers me more knowing that I'm giving up on my dream. I'm giving up on freedom. There will be no trip to the New York Public Library. I won't check out a thousand books on every subject under the sun. I won't do anything but exactly what he commands.

Hades holds out a pen, thick and black and shiny. "Make your choice."

Why is he doing this? It—it was almost easier when he didn't give me one. Now I'm confronted with all of it again. Decker. My mother. My own body, betraying me. The cruelest, most beautiful man I've ever seen sits across his desk from me, watching with ice in his eyes. I squeeze my eyes closed and force myself to picture it. Being thrown out onto the mountain in bare feet, the rocks cutting into my flesh. The dull snap of Decker's neck, if he's still alive, and his body falling to the floor. My mother's wrath. A pointless dream.

Everything I've done will be for nothing.

"I don't want to belong to you," I tell him. This might be the last moment I can say this.

He smiles. "Too late."

"Give me the pen," I whisper.

As I reach for it, I glance up into Hades' face one more time and catch an expression I'd never thought I'd see—relief. He narrows his eyes and it disappears. Relief? What could he have to be relieved about? And what would it have to do with me?

I don't ask any questions. I know better than that. I just take the pen and sign my name.

It's done.

14

PERSEPHONE

THE MOMENT I put the papers back on the table, everything changes.

Hades stands, towering over me, and leans down to put his own signature below mine. It's a manly scrawl that runs over mine in places, as if he doesn't really care where mine ends and his begins.

"They're ready," he calls. The man must've been standing outside the door all along, because takes him no time at all to collect the papers from Hades' hands. "File them with the rest. Get up."

It takes me a moment too long to rise from my seat, which earns me a scowl that makes goosebumps rise up and down my back. *What now?* I allow myself to think it. I don't allow myself to say it. The rest of me quakes as I stand waiting for Hades to do...whatever it is he's going to do. There's not enough air in the room. Now is when it happens, isn't it? Now is when he takes whatever it is that he wants from me. Whatever's left. I steel myself for a hand around my throat and close my eyes. Soon, he'll grab me there, and then...then he'll be in charge. I won't have to think about this anymore. I'll just let it happen.

But the only thing that brushes against my exposed throat is a shift in the air as he moves past me, Conor at his heels. They wait at the door.

"Come here *now*." I stub my toe on the chair leg in my hurry to get to him. My heart beats so hard and fast it's like a horse given its head for the first time, racing across an open field. The dress—nightgown—whatever it is—rides up. It's hard to keep it down in place and follow him at the same time. We take one hallway down to the big open area at the center of his private rooms and make another turn. Down another long hallway. At the end of the hall is a set of double doors, but he doesn't go through them. He stops at another door, a single one, right before it.

Hades opens the door with the air of a man who has run out of time and patience.

"Go in."

This time, I don't hesitate. I'm a little proud of that.

"Your personal maid will be here soon. Don't go farther than the end of the hall."

He turns to leave.

"Wait." I'm still turning when I catch Hades by the sleeve and he pauses, staring down at my hand like I've shocked him. My heart has gone off-rhythm. I drop my hand and draw myself up to my full height, though I still feel unsteady. It was one thing to throw myself at him when Decker was dangling from his hands. It's another to have our names scrawled together on what looks like a very official document. I don't know what he plans to do with it, but dread pools at the base of my belly. "Where are you going?"

Hades looks at me, blue eyes questioning.

"I have business. Did you think I'd be spending every waking moment with you?"

His fingers in my hair, his laughter in my ears, *did you think you were special?*

Yes. "No."

He comes back across the threshold.

"Is this some kind of admission, Persephone? Are you admitting you need supervision in order to hold up your end of the agreement?"

My end of the agreement is to be here. Submission without limits. What else could I do?

"That's not what I'm—no." I only thought that you would keep me with you. I should be crying tears of joy right now, or tears of relief, if he's willing to leave me alone. After the morning I've had the last thing I should crave is a rough man's touch. "I wondered. That's all."

"You didn't wonder anything of the kind, that much is clear." He's taken up all the space between us, compressing the air down to nothing. "If you'd thought at all you wouldn't be wasting my time."

"What was the morning for, then?" My voice rises, getting away from me. "You left me in that room with those people—"

"With Genie and her team." It sounds like scolding, and it pisses me off. "You needed their services."

"They took my dress, and my clothes. Now I only have this, and you're—you're leaving?"

Hades puts his hands in his pockets, a heated expression playing slowly across his lips, making its way to his eyes.

"Are you angry because they made you into something tolerable or because I didn't bother to inspect their work?"

"You don't need to inspect—"

That's all I get out before his hand comes down over my mouth, huge and immovable. He turns me as easily as a doll, walking me into the room and over to a four-poster bed. It's the biggest bed I've ever seen. Compared to the twin mattresses we had at home, it's huge. But Hades doesn't use the space there. He marches me over to one of the posts and snatches both wrists in one of his hands.

"Up here. That's it, sweetheart. Keep them up there if you'd rather avoid a punishment." He laughs, the sound wicked and dark. "Though, if you insist on it, I can always rearrange my schedule."

I gasp in a breath against his hand and then it's gone, leaving my lips open to the air. Words bubble up, a hundred questions, a jagged pulse of anxiety, but before I can speak a length of cloth covers my mouth and slips between my teeth. A gag. Hades tugs it tight behind my head, sounding satisfied at his handiwork. When he's got it tied off he gives it a cruel twist and I cry out against the cloth.

"That's better." He strokes down the back of my neck, lifting the extra fabric away from my skin so he can blow a breath against my spine. "Now that you can't get yourself into trouble with that mouth of yours, you'll finally be able to relax."

I let out a wild laugh. Relax? Like this? Holding onto the post of the bed like it could possibly save me? I won't relax. I would never be able to.

"Now. You were upset that I didn't pause to appreciate Genie's work. You're right about one thing—she does excellent work, even on tough cases like you." He reaches down and jerks up the hem of the nightgown. It's thin, unsubstantial, but having it raised lets the slowly circulating air caress the naked skin underneath. I have nothing left to protect me. Nothing to keep me from him. He can see everything. Hades twists it into itself so it stays lodged at my shoulders. This is so much worse than being naked. I'd rather be naked. No—I wouldn't. At least he's letting me keep this. Which is it? Why can't I decide?

He gives a sharp slap to the back of my thighs.

"You know better than that."

At first I don't know what he's talking about, what he could possibly be talking about, and then I realize that I've clamped my thighs together so hard the muscles are already trembling. I manage to inch my feet apart, caught between wanting to avoid the punishment he'd be so happy to give me and wanting to cling to the very last shreds of my modesty. There are practically none left. I don't know why it matters, only that it does.

Hades has no patience for this. He pushes one foot between my legs and shoves them apart. Wide. Conor makes a sound, almost disapproving, and appears at my side. *My* side. Hades turns my face to the side so the dog can see.

"I'm not hurting her," he snaps. "She's *fine*." Is this what *fine* is? Hades snaps his fingers. "Go lay down." Conor grudgingly pulls away. He finds a fireplace. My heart slows a little bit.

"Keep your legs here. Do you understand?"

I nod frantically, feeling the tears leak one by one out from under my eyes. Only—I'm not crying out of fear. I'm not even sure why it's happening. I could be wrong. It could be fear. Maybe I've stopped feeling it. Maybe this last day has done that to me. Maybe he's done that to me. Hades works a hand down over my ass and squeezes.

"Good." His hand is slightly rough and calloused. Every ridge is obvious against my skin as he tests my other asscheek, then unceremoniously spreads them apart. I lean my forehead against the post of the bed and try to keep breathing. My stomach sinks down to my toes, knees weakening. It's hard to keep my legs spread like this. My thighs ache from the position. He's looking at me. He's looking at me there. I thought it was bad before, in the elevator, when he touched me. That was nothing.

The moment goes on and on, stretching out into eternity.

Hades is being awful.

And the longer it goes on, the weaker my knees get. A strange warmth arcs across my chest, twisting itself up with an ache that feels like wanting. The drop of shame melds with a fluttering anticipation until it's hard to tell one sickness from another. This can't be happening.

He strokes one finger over my most sensitive, secret place. My head falls back and a sound escapes me, a sound so sultry I don't even recognize my own voice.

Hades rewards this by letting go and grabbing one of my hips with another light slap.

"You are a fucking liar," he murmurs in my ear, the heat of his body covering my back. "You're such a wide-eyed, innocent little liar." One of his hands comes up to grip my jaw, pulling the gag even tighter. "I'd say I would train it out of you, but that would be such a waste." His lips brush my cheek, which is wet with my tears. He braces my head against his chest, or somewhere near his shoulder, I don't know—all I know is that I'm still upright, and it's a miracle.

Then his other hand traces a path to the front of me, circling each nipple with the sharp edge of his nail. I can't stop the sounds any more than I could let go of the post. *This is wrong, this is wrong, this is wrong.* The chant goes around in circles in my mind until it's a meaningless song.

His hand moves downward.

Inch by inch by inch.

He circles my belly button.

He goes lower.

I can't breathe.

I'm doing nothing but breathing, sucking in air through the fabric between my teeth. The sound is harsh compared to Hades' even breathing.

His hand stops moving.

He's inches away from my clit. It throbs just from the proximity, painful and wanting and bad, it's bad. It's so bad. The prickling sense of being in trouble runs over my skin like a cascade of hot water, dropped from above by a woman in a dark uniform. I wish he would touch me. Please, *please* touch me. Bring an end to this torturous anticipation. The waiting is the worst thing by far. My knuckles tighten on the bedpost.

He doesn't move his hand.

He's so close, the buttons of his jacket brushing against my spine, but he keeps his fingers splayed low on my belly.

Why?

He waits.

Hades is the king of waiting, that's what he is. He pretends he has no patience, but he has enough to torture me. What does he want? What do I have to do to get him to touch me, to finish this? I am already arched backward, hips thrust out toward the bedpost, body bent for him. But I push them out another inch further.

"It's terrible, what I'm doing to do." That voice in my ear is enough to make my knees give out, but I don't let it. "Do you remember, Persephone? I promised I'd make you beg."

But I can't beg. I can't say anything, not with this gag in my mouth. The whimpering sound I make next embarrasses me more than everything that's come before it.

"Please. Of course you can beg. You've done it just now. Only that's not enough for me to give you what you want. It's not enough for me to give you anything you want." His lips brush against the side of my neck—the shadow of a kiss. "I could decide to give you something you want. It wouldn't go against our agreement."

Another sound. I can't stop it. And the heat and want have grown so powerful that my mind clouds, hiding the sharp mortification of this moment behind something dirty and hot. No, I can't do this. I can't give into him. It's very, very bad, and it's very wrong.

It's not up to me now. It's not my rational mind that moves my hips again, rolling them forward. I can't move far. I can't move much. But it's enough. I do it again, and again. It's obscene. I'm fucking the air, with his hand on me and his gag in my mouth and my name on his papers. It's the worst thing I've ever done.

He slips two fingers down between my legs, down into the wetness that's already waiting for him, and pulls them back up to circle my clit. I'm nothing now, an animal, a bundle of nerves that don't know what to do with themselves. The noise that comes out of me is barely human and if anyone ever heard it, it would be the end of me. But Hades hears it, and his hand goes still.

"No," I cry into the gag, but it's muffled and distorted.

"If you want more, you'll have to get it yourself." He sounds completely detached. "You'll have to admit that you want it. You'll have to prove that you want this."

And god help me, I do.

I work my hips up into his hand, legs spread wide, dripping down my own thighs. Sweat beads on my forehead. I can't let go of the post. I can't let him let go of me.

I'm almost there, on the brink of something obliterating, when he takes his hand away and steps back.

I howl into the gag, sagging against the bedpost.

Hades leans down over me.

"Almost, but not quite." He reaches forward and wipes his hand against my back, then presses the ghost of a kiss to my shoulder. "I almost believed you, liar." His footsteps retreat toward the door. A snap of his fingers, and Conor goes, too. "Oh—" Every cell in my being bends to him, calling him to come back across the room. "Not Genie's best work. But like I said—you were a difficult case."

15

PERSEPHONE

HADES LEAVES THE ROOM.

I hear his footsteps retreating in the hall, each one softer than the last, and hold tighter to the bedpost. Surely, *surely*, he's coming back. Surely he wouldn't leave me like this. I'm nearly at death's door, only it was the most pleasant death I could have imagined. Even thinking about his touch sends new sensations zinging between my legs. I'm so focused on it that time goes by without me marking it. I couldn't have kept track if I tried, but I'm not trying, I'm busy imagining his fingers where they were and trying to get there on force of fantasy alone.

So when the footsteps come down the hall, I'm too

far gone to notice that I should be doing something other than clinging to a bedpost with my dress hiked up to my shoulders, rolled around itself, and a gag in my mouth. Like rearranging my clothes—anything. But I'm not. I'm still frustrated and overheated and lost to myself.

Where is he? Why would he do this to me? What do I have to do, run naked through the hallways to get his attention? Do I even want his attention? I'm used to dreaming of empty fields, without a single person looking at me, and now—him?

The footsteps get closer.

They're too light and too soft to be his.

But why would he leave, in the middle of that? He's a terrible man, even more terrible than I thought

The footsteps can't be his because they're so light and measured.

The footsteps can't be his.

The footsteps arrive at the doorway at the same time all the disarrayed puzzle pieces of my thoughts fit themselves together. I let go of the bedpost with a shriek and leap to the left. There's nothing to the left to hide me. The door opens, and the air moves over my skin. Dress first. Dress first. Oh my god, I can't get it down.

"Miss Persephone?"

It's definitely not him, this woman with a soft, even voice, and I burst into flame and crumble into a burnt-up husk. When the flame recedes I'm unfortunately left in my own body. Why won't the dress come untwisted? How much worse could this possibly get? Maybe she hasn't seen me. Maybe she'll just leave.

"Let me help you with that."

I blink at the bed, too frozen to turn around. Her footsteps come across the plush carpeted behind me. Every step is amplified in my newly perished state. Then a pair of gentle hands untwists the dress and tugs it back into place. She, whoever she is, smooths it down at the hem with a touch that's somehow professional in its intimacy. Next comes the gag. He tied a tight knot, no doubt to leave me in this exact situation. Frustrated tears wend their way down my cheeks. When is this going to stop? I was never a crier before. It was useless in the face of my mother.

It's not useless to Hades. He likes it.

Which makes him far worse than my mother.

Then again...

The gag comes loose and I turn around before I lose my scrap of nerve. The woman who helped me wears a long black skirt and a black vest over a white dress shirt—one of the maid's uniforms I saw on the way in. She has eyes the color of cocoa and hair a few shades lighter. The maid folds the fabric that made up the gag as delicately as she might fold something precious and delicate. It's not a precious item of clothing, I see now. It's one of Hades' ties, from around his neck. She presses it into one of her pockets—out of sight, out of mind—and looks at me with a smile that reveals nothing. A knot at the center of my collarbone untwists. Her expression is far softer than Genie's, and less afraid.

"Good morning." She extends a hand to me and we shake, like I'm not standing here in a dress that could be lingerie and she didn't just help me hide my naked ass. "My name is Lillian. I'll be your personal assistant." She wrinkles her nose. "I think that has a nicer ring to it than *maid*. Though some of the people around here don't think so."

I drop my hands back in front of me. "You already know my name, I think."

She nods slowly. "I do. But I don't know anything else about you. Not much information was provided when I was reassigned. Come this way, and tell me what you like to drink with your breakfast. Tea? Coffee?" Lillian drops her voice. "I'm sure I could sneak you a mimosa once every so often."

Reassigned from *where*? How many other household staff does Hades have, and where do they work? Who are they working for? Does he have other women here? The questions explode like fireworks at the front of my mind across a dark backdrop of jealousy. I let them fizzle out without saying anything.

A...mimosa?

Is she joking?

"Anything but herbal tea." If I have to keep drinking herbal tea, then I'd rather close my eyes and depart from the world. My mother didn't believe in caffeine. Rising at dawn, yes. Caffeine, no. Fresh morning air—that's the thing I'll miss. The dew beneath my feet. The soft calls of birds.

None of that is available here. "I've had coffee a few times, and I liked it."

She's still wearing a small, sly grin, as if the two of us are close friends and she doesn't work for the man who... owns me. He as good as owns me. Lillian doesn't go far. She leads me across the room toward a hallway that's narrower than the one outside this room, but not by much. The lights adjust for us as we reach the threshold and go down the hall.

Lillian puts her hand flat against the first door on the right. "This is your closet. I'll take care of it for you. If there's anything you ever need, all you have to do is tell me, and I'll have it repaired or replaced depending on your preference." Another door, on the left. "The bathroom."

"This is a suite, not—not a separate bedroom, or a —" I don't remember anything about a suite on the contract. Every breath I take erases more of the words on the page from my mind. Fear is a slippery thing. It puts itself between you and everything you think you should know, and it pops up again and again, like a hydra that never loses all its heads. "I thought..."

"You thought you might be kept down in some empty cell?"

I whip my head around to look at her, blood fleeing from my lips, leaving them numb and buzzing. "Does he do that?" I'm thinking of Decker, wishing I could run to wherever he is. Wishing I could put my hands on his face and make sure he's still drawing breaths. I'm thinking of myself, too. "Are there...people in a dungeon here?"

Her eyes search mine and she nods, the movement barely there. "A place of this size has to have somewhere for people to be...kept. If necessary." Lillian reaches down, takes my hand, and gives it a brief squeeze. "If it's any consolation, I don't think that's where you're headed. Mr. Hades isn't in that kind of business."

"What kind of business?"

She presses her lips together. "How much do you know about him?"

"I know he's ruthless." One word slips out, then another, until they become a stream I can't stop. "I know he's mean." My eyes fill with tears. "My mother always told me that if he ever found me, he'd kill me. I never knew why. I still don't know why. I just know that he's the kind of man who could take someone's life without even thinking about it. Without even a second of regret." Pain presses in on my lungs until it's hard to take a full breath. "I shouldn't be telling you this at all." I turn my face away and wipe the back of my hand across my cheeks, swiping away the tears. "You're—you work for him." Another surge of horror. "You might go and repeat back everything I've said, and then—"

Lillian takes both of my hands and squeezes hard. Hard enough that I let out a yelp. Her dark eyes look like thunderstorms in miniature. The pain clears my head, makes it easier to breathe. She drops my hands.

"I do work for Mr. Hades," she says softly. "But I'm assigned to you. I'm your personal assistant. I can do your hair, get you something to eat. Whatever you need." Lillian laughs lightly. "Basically my job is to keep you happy." She screws up her lips. "Listen. I won't tell your secrets. My job is to help you, not spy on you."

The look on her face makes me laugh. "I hope not.

Since I just told you a bunch of...highly personal information."

"Is there anything else that's bothering you?" She widens her dark eyes, the picture of concern. "Because we can talk about it, if you want." Lillian glances back toward the main bedroom, toward the door. It's closed. No sign of anyone approaching. "I won't say anything."

A worry that's burrowed itself down in the center of my gut blooms. Should I tell her? Should I say anything? Because if she's lying, then Hades will hear every word. I saw him last night. He could retaliate and it would all be over. But it could all be over anyway, and I have no way of knowing if this is for nothing. It makes a difference. Even if my promises are written in ink and set in stone, it makes a difference.

"There is something." My heart pounds, pulse so loud in my ears that for a moment I can't hear my own breath. "I'm not sure if there's anything that can be done, anything that you—" The words get choked off by fear. I swallow it back. "I'm here because..." How do I explain this to another person, much less a woman who's getting paid to be with me by Hades himself? I start again. "I made a deal. A...trade. A man I was with..." A flare of anger almost succeeds at burning through my fear, but not quite. What the hell was Decker doing, going into that train car? Why couldn't he just have stuck to the plan? He was always so worried that I wouldn't stick to the plan, that I'd mess something up by taking matters into my own hands, and now look at us.

Well...look at me. Maybe he's already been buried under the ground and I didn't save him after all. The thought of all that dirt pressing down on him makes me feel like I've been buried, too. It extinguishes my anger and replaces it with a creeping sadness, like a lungful of water.

"Did he cross Mr. Hades?" Lillian prompts. There's no sting in her voice, but I sense a certain urgency. She's right. If Hades comes back in the middle of this conversation I can't imagine it will go well. "Was that the trade?"

"I traded myself to save him," I say quickly. "The last I saw, some of Hades' men were dragging him away. I don't know if they put him on the train with us, or—or where he went." Or if they slit his throat. Or if they snapped his neck and left his body in the woods by the tracks. Or if they hauled him here and threw him off the mountain. It's better not to think of it. Thinking of it makes my balance weak and unreliable. "Is there any way—"

"I'll see what I can find out." Lillian gives me an encouraging smile. "And don't worry. Your secret is my secret, and I don't tell secrets."

I blow out a breath, trying to slow my racing heart. Should I have taken the risk? It's too late now.

Lillian pats down the apron she wears over her black dress. "There's one more room to show you. Would you like to see it now, or later?"

I want to move. "Now is good. Please, show me now."

She moves down the hall toward the final door at the end of the hall and opens it. Every heartbeat is ready to burst out of my veins and explode me into nothing. I've seen what kinds of rooms Hades has. I have no doubt this will be another place where he can have people...do things to me. Or do them himself.

"Miss?"

"Please," I say automatically. "Call me Persephone." It's only once I've spoken that I realize I've been squeezing my eyes shut. They're only open enough to keep me from running face-first into a wall.

"Persephone." Lillian's voice coaxes me into opening them all the way. "This is the library."

16

HADES

THE DIAMOND MINES are the farthest I can get from Persephone. They also happen to be the closest source of people who require correction in any number of ways. But stalking through the mines doesn't help the burning in my blood. It does nothing to tame this...*emotion* stampeding through my veins. An intolerable emotion. One that grows with every second that passes. The morning bleeds by, then the afternoon, and evening. As much as I relish the terror in their eyes, there is, unfortunately, a limit. There's a limit for me, too, though none of them will ever know that. I stay until Conor shoves me in the direction of the exits, away from the floodlights that keep the work illuminated. I can feel the effects of it beginning at the far reaches of my mind. If it gets worse—

I'm not fucking thinking about what happens when it gets worse. Not now.

The main thing is that I don't want to pull my whole fucking enterprise down on my own head. What a waste it would be—all those painstaking deals, all that insolence crushed beneath my heel. All of that can't come to nothing.

Not today.

The news of my mood has clearly spread through the staff. All of them scurry out of my path on the way back to my private wing. Not one of those cowards is in sight by the time I get inside.

I slam the door to my office and pace behind my desk. Back out toward the door. Back to the desk. If I had less self-control, I'd pull everything off the shelves and rip it apart. I need the destruction like I need air and water.

What happened in that room—it could be my undoing, as much as it is hers.

I've touched Persephone before. It should have been as meaningless as it's ever been, with every other woman I've taken to my bed. But it wasn't. It fucking wasn't. And I don't know whether it was the press of her head against my chest or the sounds she made with my fingers on her naked flesh. I don't know if it was the way she looked completely clothed as part of my household, not a stitch on her from anywhere else. She tried so fucking hard to please me, and not only because she was afraid.

I *saw* her.

Fuck.

Persephone is right to be afraid. I'm a dangerous man. I'm not dangerous to *her*, at least not in the way that makes her tremble. I won't hurt her any more than is pleasurable. I could never kill her. I know it now, in stark black and white.

I sit down heavily behind the desk and run my hands over my face, then slap my hand down on the switch that controls the lights in the room. It's gotten bad today. Worse than ever before. The two lamps in my office still have the last of the low-wattage bulbs. They're the only ones I haven't replaced. They'll have to go. I curl up a hand into a fist and stop myself from smashing them.

In the dark I let my eyes settle. Conor pushes his

nose against my knee, then rests his head on top of my thigh. I don't have to see to lean back in my chair and continue controlling myself moment by moment. And I don't have to see to answer my cell phone when it rings.

"What?"

"I need you to search the mountain." Zeus sounds like he's walking fast, and I don't care at all where he's going. "Persephone's not anywhere in the city, as far as I can tell, and I have people everywhere."

"I love when you call me to make demands," I croon into the phone. "Especially when you know it's pointless. She's not here."

"There are only a few places she could have gone." My brother's voice is harried. "If she left on the train, then—"

"Listen to yourself." I tip my head back and close my eyes, hating how fucking useless it makes me feel. I take that feeling by the throat and crush it until I can't feel it anymore. I want him to keep her name out of his mouth. I want him to lose my number, forget my name. "The girl left, did she not? It's none of my business if a grown woman wants to leave her mother's house. And frankly, you obnoxious asshole, I don't see why you care at all."

"Don't *you*?" Now he's incredulous, and I can almost see his handsome face contorted into disbelief. "You of all people should have a stake in this."

"I have other priorities." The desk was built to withstand me. It doesn't budge when I brace my hand against it and push until the wood threatens to cut into my palm. "This matter doesn't concern me. And now you've brought it up twice in one day. If it's that important to you, then come here in person."

Zeus has never set foot here. He calls it the Underworld, and the nickname became so pervasive that eventually I had to take control of it myself. The worthless fucker. Always with his hands and his dick where they don't belong, causing chaos wherever he goes.

"I might have to, if you're going to be so unhelpful."

"Unhelpful?" I laugh at him. I know he hates it, so I let him hear exactly how much I'm enjoying it. "Your little empire in the city would be nothing without me. Are you sure you want to upset our special relationship just because Demeter's daughter stepped out?"

This will have gotten him where it hurts. He hates to admit that our businesses have a mutual dependence, though on my end it's more out of convenience than anything else. But he needs me. The city needs me, even if they'll never admit it out loud.

"If you don't want me to pay a visit, then come to the city. I have some men here who might give me more information if you become involved."

Zeus wants to play the good man in every equation. My lip curls, disgust welling up from an endless supply. If he wasn't hiding such a disgusting personality, I might find something in him to admire. But it's only a convenient disguise. A handsome face and a trap, all in one. I don't want him here. I have no plans to ever let him into my private quarters, but there's no telling what he might try with my staff. If he came here, there's a chance, however small...

"I'm not agreeing to anything.

"Neither is Demeter. She's come a little...unhinged."

A chill creeps along the base of my spine, and Conor growls. Persephone has only been with me a matter of hours. If Zeus is lying to get under my skin, then it's best not to react in the slightest. But if he's telling the truth, things could get personally uncomfortable for me. I grind my teeth together.

"Again, this is entirely useless information." It's the most important information I've ever received. My hackles are up, the hairs on the back of my neck standing straight out. It would be easier to tell if Zeus was lying if I could see him in person. He probably knows that. Under any other circumstance, I wouldn't care what Zeus is pretending to know. But the stakes are higher now. Zeus. Demeter. Me, with Persephone here, down the hall in that scrap of lingerie. A tangled fucking web indeed.

"Come to the city and help me." I hate Zeus, I truly do. "It'll only take a day or two."

I laugh out loud. "You think it would take me two days to extract information from some weak asshole? It wouldn't take me two hours."

Zeus chuckles, like we're two brothers sharing a pleasant moment, and I glare at the opposite wall.

"Then come enjoy the city. I'll get you some women. Maybe it would improve your mood."

Acid burns the back of my throat. No. *Fuck* no. I don't want any of Zeus's women, or the restaurants he goes to so people can fawn over him like a handsome prince. But what is the alternative? He can't come here. I'd have to kill him before I let him set foot this close to Persephone. I wouldn't mind killing Zeus. I would mind the general upheaval that would follow, in that it would be the kind of distraction that's impossible to ignore.

I want to squeeze this phone until it shatters, but that would be two in one day. Self-control, Luther. Self-control.

"I'll come if I have time." I hang up before he can answer and toss the phone onto the desk. It skids to the edge and falls to the carpet.

The silence of the office without Zeus' voice is welcome after the clashes and clangs of the mines. Welcome for a moment, anyway. One moment flows into the next and for a while it's relatively peaceful. Then my mind catches on image after image. Tears spilling from Persephone's eyes. Her trembling body under my hands. The sway of her hips while she crawled across the floor. No amount of denying myself can keep them away. I want her. I want her too much to sit here, but I keep my feet firmly planted on the floor and my hands against the edge of the desk. The mountain moves around me, alive with people whose movements feel like ants in an anthill. All of them running to do my bidding. Only one of them matters. Down in the mines, the evening crew comes on, pickaxes ready to carve out gemstones from the rock. And Persephone waits.

I don't know how long it's been when I finally stand up. The hall on the way to my most private rooms is still and empty, the way it should be. There's a certain pleasure in the late hours, when it could be any time at all. The night is liquid on the way to my sanctuary within a sanctuary. Even if Zeus came here, I would never let him into my private apartment. A fortress within a home within a fortress. Some people might label this paranoia. But I live every day with the knowledge that anything brave and strong enough to kill me is an earnest threat.

The silence deepens as I get closer to my bedroom suite and send Conor in ahead of me. The night attendant will let him in and make sure he's fed. It's a deep enough silence for a thought to occur to me —maybe she escaped. There is only one way to escape from here. I did, after all, leave her in a room with considerable furnishings. Something like fear grips my throat. It's such a foreign sensation that I try to rub it away.

The door to her suite opens beneath my hand as easily as it ever has, the turn of the handle as soundless as the room within. For a few moments I can't hear anything.

Then—

Even breathing.

Persephone sleeps in a circle of light from the bedside lamp, almost hidden from view by the hangings at the head of the bed. Her small frame blends with the pillows and the blankets.

She's surrounded by books.

Neat stacks of two or three, perhaps fifteen in total, are fanned out around her. She holds one under her arm, like she fell asleep reading it. My heart tugs at the sight of it and I rear back, turning away.

What the hell, what the *hell.*

She looks so defenseless, so vulnerable, so young. And the feeling that sloshes through me, messy and uncontained, is one of tenderness.

Fuck me.

I can't feel tenderness toward her. Or anyone. Ever.

My own dark needs come thundering in a moment late for this fucking party. It's a relief—that surge of violent energy. I don't want to caress her, I want to spank her. Or maybe it's both. I don't want to let her sleep. I want to haul her out of the bed, shove her dress up to her waist, and cover her mouth while she cries underneath me. I don't want to deny myself any longer. I want to take her now, with thrusts that will make her feel so alive it hurts, and then hurts again, until there's nothing left but me inside of her.

It's absurd, and I loathe it—more than I loathe Zeus, more than I loathe my deal with Demeter, more than I loathe the endless dance of keeping people in their places. She's so fucking close. I turn back around and look at her again. She does not sense me here. If she did, those eyes would open wide, and she'd know to be afraid.

It's another man, who isn't me, or who isn't *all* me, who stands up straight.

Who walks around to the other side of the bed and reaches over her to pluck the book from under her arm.

Who considers it, stifling a laugh. I had them set the library for a woman while we were on the train. This is the kind of thing she'd like—of course it is. It's the kind of thing Demeter would never let her read. It goes on the bedside table.

It's another man who pulls the blanket up around her shoulders and turns out the light.

And it's another man who closes the door tightly behind him and goes to his own room, without touching her at all.

17

PERSEPHONE

THE DOOR TO MY ROOM—MY suite—opens with a breath of air, and Lillian comes in with her silver tray, dark eyes alight.

Breakfast on a silver tray, the way she has every morning for the last three mornings.

Without Hades.

She gives me a warm smile, eyes flicking over me. I'm already awake, just under the covers with a book. Waiting for him.

"Good morning, Persephone." Lillian makes her way to the side of the bed and positions the tray over my lap like we've stepped right into one of the historical books from Hades' library and I'm the lady of the house. "Did you sleep well?"

"Yes, of course." *No.* I woke up several times, thinking I heard him in the room. I lay the book next to me, touching my thigh so I can be sure of its continued existence. My heart beats faster now that she's close. Now that I have the chance to ask the only question that matters. Every morning, I find different ways to ask it.

Lillian goes over to the curtains by the window and draws them open, one by one, letting a bit of light in. Like everywhere else in Hades' home, it's a strange light. It makes me miss the sun. He must hate the daylight so much that he can't even allow it in his windows in diluted form.

"Is there...anything scheduled for today that I should know about?"

The set of Lillian's shoulders—relaxed and easy—tells me before she speaks that no, there's nothing on any sort of schedule. The only schedule that could possibly matter is the one Hades' sets for me. I guess I can imagine him telling his plans to Lillian for the express purpose of making my face turn red and hot.

"Not that I know of." She's constantly on the move, gently transforming the room around me. Straightening the hangings on the bed. Moving a stray book from the chair by the window to the table by my elbow. I don't keep much in the suite—I don't have much to keep—but somehow, when she's made her rounds back to the door, it looks fresh and new. "Are you reading this morning?"

I smile back at her, but it's only to cover the frustration twisting and turning like a creature wending its way through my ribs and settling between my thighs. Where is he? Where did he go? The questions are steam in a tea kettle, waiting for its chance to scream.

"Until something happens." I drum my fingertips on the covers of the book.

Lillian leaves with a swish of her black skirt and the whisper of the door closing behind her. I manage the coffee, which is a revelation. Sugar and cream changes the color to a delicate tan. The food is...fine.

Half a piece of toast later, I've abandoned my breakfast to the tray and the tray to the bed. The book fails to hold my attention. I start again. How much would I have given to have unfettered access to this many books in my mother's house? I'd have given a lot. Maybe a change of scenery would help. But even the library can't compete with my insatiable need to *know*. The answers aren't in this book, or any of the others. It's just more frustration—frustration I shouldn't even be feeling.

I. Should. Not. Miss. Him.

And I don't. I don't miss him. That's not it, not exactly. What it is, exactly...

Unfinished business.

An unfinished orgasm, for one thing. That's at the top of my list. I wander back out into the main room and gaze out the window, not seeing the harsh drop down the side of the mountain at all. How could he leave me like that? Was it supposed to be a kindness or a punishment? The odds of Hades doing anything resembling a kindness are slim, so it must have been the other option. He must be trying to torture me. He must know, somehow, that I've been lying under my sheets for the past few nights with flushed cheeks and a clenched jaw and all of my efforts have come to nothing but lost sleep.

Now I do focus on the mountainside, the wall

jutting out of it and the drop into misty nothingness. The wide sill is the perfect place to brace my hands so I can press my forehead to the cool glass. I stare until my vision blurs, but it still doesn't erase the tightly wound feeling at the apex of my legs, pulsing and begging, god, it's relentless.

"If you're going to bend over like that, you should do it naked."

His voice hits first, and then a chill in the room, like he's come in out of the cold and it's sticking to his skin. Then the heat. Heat in my face, heat between my legs, heat streaking down my chest like a lightning bolt. I whirl around, forgetting the obscenely short length of the nightgown, letting the silky robe hang open.

Hades stands in the doorway, looking at me like he owns every part of me. He has Conor with him. He always does, and I guess he probably always will. But he doesn't own every part. I'll always hold something back from him, I will. I have to, for Decker, if only in memory of him. I'm here for *Decker*, for my love of Decker, the first person to risk his own job and his own security to make me laugh. I'm not here for me. But the words banging at the floodgates of my mind spring through.

"Where have you been?"

It's not a smile that crosses his face—something similar, but harder. It cuts. "Sharing my whereabouts with you isn't part of our agreement."

"But we have an agreement. Arrangement. Whatever you want to call it." My head throbs, my throat tightens, I could combust. "You've been gone for days, with no word." His lip curls. A sneer? The flicker of expression is gone before I can name it. "I've been...here. You left me in the middle of—" I can't bring myself to say it. "I don't even know if you've kept up your end of the bargain." Hades wears a perfect suit. His shoes are perfectly shined. There is nothing about him that speaks to flaws, and I feel like a crumbling wreck. "I don't even know if Decker is still alive."

He takes one step into the room and all of me goes still. Waiting. He signals for Conor to wait at the door. The dog doesn't take a single step inside.

"You bargained for his life in a... particular instance. That doesn't mean I have to spare him indefinitely." He waves this off. "But if you're insisting that I haven't been honorable, then let's go to my office."

A trap—it has to be a trap. He is not honorable. Hades has never even pretended to be an honorable man. Another swarm of thoughts to the same effect sweeps across my brain. Let's go to my office. A threat.

He claps his hands, once, the sound sharp.

"Don't make me wait."

My bravery flees. All that pent-up energy drops to the floor, then springs back up in another form. What was I thinking, talking to him like that? What if I've tipped the scales into something worse? It freezes me in place, barefoot in my robe.

Hades curses under his breath and strides across the room. Every step he takes makes him loom larger and larger until he's right on top of me. I was right before—he does smell cold, like a winter wind. He bends down low, threading his hand through my hair, and pulls until I have no choice but to look at him and my eyes sting with tears.

"My favorite sight." His fist tightens in my curls. "I missed you. Now move."

What else am I supposed to do, other than stumble forward? Nothing. My feet go numb, clumsy. His legs are so much longer than mine. He is so much more powerful. And I am so, so scared. The only way to avoid being dragged is to keep up, and I try. I try my best. I try so hard that at first I don't notice that we've gone past the big door to his private office.

I haven't been outside his private space for days, and the hall outside is huge in comparison. He's built himself a palace fortress, with layers inside layers, all of them as impenetrable as he is.

It's not quiet out here. Conor's nails on the floor are the backdrop to a chorus of other sounds. The closer we get toward that big rotunda, the more people there are. I feel them seeing me as acutely as I feel his fist in my hair and the cooler air of the hall slipping under my dress—my nightgown—the clothes. The *clothes*. The delicate lace underthings I found in the closet, all of them looking like he could shred them under his hands. I blink away tears. Some of them escape and evaporate off my skin.

Hades takes me through the center of the rotunda, his footsteps echoing louder than any of the others. A path opens up for us wherever we go. A wide space. An empty space. No one dares touch him, or touch me. He barks an order at someone, but I can't hear it through the haze of the pain.

A set of doors opens and we cross over the threshold. A large room. Flashes of leather and steel. A wide glass desk. And the most massive windows I've ever seen. Hades releases his grip, only slightly, only so I can straighten up and see where we are.

His office. His real office. And his office overlooks...

An enormous factory floor. His hand goes around the back of my neck and I lurch forward again, following him through another set of doors. Conor stays where he is. He must know this play already.

The sound is like nothing I've ever heard. It's an enormous, relentless sound, an echo off the impossibly high ceilings and a storm made up of all the work that goes on below us. Rows of work tables line a room bigger than some of my mother's fields. It's not a space that should fit indoors, and yet...it does. It is. He's made the impossible absolutely real. At the far end of the room is a yawning chasm, a rip in the rock. From here I can make out a line of people in a constant stream. I blink in the face of the noise. The steady beat of machines. A foreman's voice, rising above the fray. Tools on metal.

And a deeper hum. Mining. They're mining something, over in that tear.

He pushes me to the railing. This is more than a balcony, it's a viewing platform, and the waist-high wall is made of glass. We're high above the people below. But not that high. High enough that a drop wouldn't kill me. High enough that if they looked up, they could see every bit of me through the glass.

I suck in one ragged breath after another. "What—what—"

"Isn't it gorgeous?" Hades' voice sounds like a murmur against all the noise in the room. This is the sound of him pulling his power right from the earth. All his money, all his power. "Everyone down there is working for me. Everything they do is for me. And you're one of them, too. Only your work isn't with jewelry and metal and all the other things people want to buy."

There's a commotion at the other end of the room, near the enormous hole in the wall. My stomach drops. Hades traces a path around to the front of my collarbone, then clamps his hand around the front of my neck. I can't take my eyes off the people below us. They're noticing, one by one, pale faces glancing up and then back down again.

"Here he comes."

It takes them several minutes to cross the space—Decker, and the two people who have him by the arms. I always thought he looked so tall and strong, but from here he looks like a lanky teenager. Dirty. Pale-faced. Dust stains his white t-shirt, making it gray and black. One of the men with him forces his head up.

When our eyes meet, my legs would give out if it weren't for Hades with his hand around my throat, pinning me back toward his body. Every inch of him is as hard as the rocks making up his palace walls. My body struggles for a moment, unthinking, and he only holds me closer.

"There. See? He's alive. I've even given him work to do. Tell me how generous I am, Persephone. Say it."

"You're—you're very generous."

"I'm even more honorable and generous than you think. Do you know why?"

I shake my head.

"I'm going to prove to your little plaything that you're alive, too."

Hades steps back, putting space between us, and I feel like I'm dangling in midair as much as Decker was that night. But instead of pulling my feet from the ground, he pulls the robe from my shoulders. The dress goes next, along with all the air from my lungs. The fabric pulls against my skin as it tears beneath his hands and flutters to the floor at my feet. I'm up here in front of his entire factory, in front of a room humming with men, in a pair of lace panties and a bralette that barely covers anything.

"While we're here, we can address your other complaint."

"I didn't have another complaint. I didn't say anything." Does he even hear me above the din?

He does.

"You were unhappy I left off in the middle of our activities the other night. If you haven't been furiously trying to get yourself off every night..." He laughs. "I'd be shocked. Ah—yes. So you have."

The heat in my face must give me away, but I don't

know how he can tell anything. My entire body feels scarlet. I'm practically naked. There are so many people. And worst of all, Decker. His eyes burn up at me from the factory floor.

Hades jerks me back against him at the same moment he steps up to the railing. His left hand is almost lovingly around my throat, putting just enough pressure to keep me in my place. And with his other hand—

He touches me.

The hollow of my collarbone. My cleavage. When he slides a hand under the bralette a strangled cry floats above the noise. Both nipples, already peaked, feel exquisitely sensitive—he pinches one, then the other. He goes lower. I can't breathe.

"Keep watching him."

I can't do anything else. Decker tries to get free, but even if he did, he couldn't get to us. One of the men holding his arms throws the first punch as Hades shoves down my panties to the center of my thighs, then strokes his fingers between my legs. Casually. Possessively. Like he's done this all his life.

My own breath catches, matching Decker's. He

can't fight those men anymore, and I can't fight Hades.

And maybe I don't want to.

One touch, and I sag against him, a wicked desire spreading outward from his fingers through every inch of me. It hurts and it's so good. It's everything I've ever felt and nothing I've ever felt.

He does it again.

"Up. Stand up." He reinforces this with a squeeze against my throat. Hades uses one leg to knock mine apart, the panties stretching to the limit. He buries his hand between my legs, stroking and pinching and god, no, god, the circles against my swollen clit. He rubs it with the knuckle of his thumb, with the pad of his thumb, with the heel of his hand.

I can't stand. I can hardly see. Everything narrows down to where his hand meets my skin. My traitorous, wanting skin.

Hades makes a noise that's half frustration, half satisfaction. Another sensation breaks through the cloud that my mind has become—him. He's hard, too. A dawning horror—is he going to fuck me in front of all these people?

The moment I have the thought is the same moment I switch to wanting it to start. It's an endless echo. If he's going to do it, do it now. If he's going to do it, let it happen right now. Right now, *right now.*

But instead he makes Decker watch.

They're all watching. How can they not be watching? Each set of eyes is another set of pinpricks. He works two thick fingers into me. My slickness helps him on his way but they feel huge, so huge, there's no way anything more than this can ever happen. Too much, too much. I try to squirm off of them and fail. All I earn is his laughter, rumbling against me.

A sob rips itself from my throat, but to my total shock, it's not because of the relentless push and spread of his fingers. Or everyone watching him do this to me. It's because I'm so desperate to come that it's tearing me in two.

Too much becomes *not enough* in a sickening instant and I find myself—I discover myself, like I'm coming upon myself in a deep wood—rocking against his hand. Begging out loud. Are they even words? I don't know, and I don't care. I'm touching him now—my hands against his hand, against my throat. Pressing harder. I want more, I want it now.

"Don't make *him* wait, you filthy thing." I'm not blinded enough that I can't see what's happening below me—that the men are waiting for Decker to make another move. That he's *going* to make another move. If I don't come. If I don't let Hades make me come in front of all these people.

His hand works harder, pushing deeper, flicking my clit with his thumb.

"Now, Persephone."

"I can't." My wail has to be loud enough for everyone to hear.

I need something else. I need, I need, I *need*—

Hades lowers his head to the curve where my neck meets my shoulder and bites.

And I come on his fingers, with his fingers inside of me, destroyed. I am destroyed. The shock waves are too powerful to stand against but he won't let me fall. All I want is to fall, but he keeps me standing, keeps me upright while I shudder and shake and cry.

When the wave subsides he's still there. He builds it again, agonizing in its slowness, in its precision. Decker remains on his feet, his face scarlet, jaw clenched. He looks like he's trying to stop himself from screaming.

He makes me come again.

It hurts more, this time.

And it also feels better.

The intensity is too much for my mind to handle, too big for my body. And I can't get away. I'm half-naked, spread open in front of all the other people he owns, I am nothing but nerves and pain and pleasure.

At the end he scoops me up like the empty shell that I am and carries me back to his rooms, back to the bed, and into a blessed dark sleep.

18

PERSEPHONE

I HEAR him in the night.

Maybe what I'm hearing is only a dream, but it hauls me bodily out of my sleep into the darkness of my room. My mind is blank for a few breaths, numb—but then the sound makes its way in.

His voice.

He's here, and close.

What night is it? How long have I been asleep?

I don't care.

The floor is cool under my feet but not cold, even though this place has been carved out of mountain rock. He must heat the floor. Even so, I pull a blanket from the chair by the window and wrap it around myself. I'm going to find him. In the sleep delirium it seems like a good idea. But how asleep am I, really? I'm not. I'm awake, just tired. Just worn out from...what happened.

Decker saw that happen.

I pad across the floor and open the bedroom suite, then listen.

The voice wasn't a dream. He's here. But I have to blink my eyes several times to be sure I'm seeing what I'm seeing, which is...

Light, coming from the cracked-door of his office. Not a normal yellow hue, like the lightbulbs in my mother's house. Not even candlelight. What is it? What kind of lamp makes light like that?

Why not find out now?

"Why not?" I pose the question to nobody while I go down the hall. I could be a ghost, floating above the floor, for all the sound my feet make. This is surely not a bad idea. It might even be a good idea. I watch myself from outside my body, moving down the hall, sleep-rumpled and wrapped in a blanket. I observe myself pushing open the door to Hades' private office. And then I'm slammed right back into my body, because that is the effect of looking at him. It brings me to myself.

He sits behind his desk, phone pressed to his ear. "It's a developing problem." If it weren't for the tired soreness suffusing every muscle of my body, I might be more shocked to hear it. Hades, having a problem? He raises one hand to his eyes and covers them, like they hurt. I can't imagine him feeling pain. But it looks like he does. Maybe monsters can feel pain. "I need people in the field. There's enough happening here to require my presence." Hades sits up straighter. "No."

He must sense me, because he uncovers his eyes and turns his head, all of him on high alert. It's something to see. He hasn't changed the way he's sitting, and yet he's changed everything about the way he's holding himself. Muscles tensed. Sharp blue eyes narrowed. He ends the call without saying another word and lets the phone fall to the surface of his desk with a muted clatter.

"You're awake."

I'm here now, and there's no going back, so I step further into the office. "I heard you talking."

A smile curls the corner of his lip. "And you decided to come wandering out of your room in the middle of the night?"

Something about him seems slightly softer in this timeless place between midnight and dawn. At least, I'm assuming it's between midnight and dawn. No—not softer. Not exactly. He's still as sharp and as hard as he's ever been. Isn't he?

"Yes." It seems like a good idea as any to drop into a chair across from him, so that's what I do. "I wanted to find you."

"You wanted another demonstration of how cruel and dishonorable I am?"

He's toying with me now, but I'm still too drunk on his fingers inside of me and the orgasms he stole from me, still too worn from the last three days of wondering, to care. A layer of him has been stripped away by the night.

"I wanted to know why you have a big dog." Conor snores by the fireplace, the orange light playing over his fur. "I didn't think you would have a dog."

"I have my uses for him.'

"But that's not all, is it? You don't just use him to—

to scare people. Or maybe even kill people." In the haze of the night, I have much less of a filter. "He helps you, doesn't he?"

"Nobody fucking *helps* me."

"I think he does."

"What else do you think?" Hades' face has gone hard, but when he glances over to where Conor sleeps, the hint of softness appears at the very edges of his expression. "Do you want to keep pushing me until you get the punishment you want? Or do you want to shut that pretty mouth of yours before you get into trouble?"

"No. What I wanted to say…" I don't want to say *anything.* I only want to *do*. "You kept your promise." Guilt tumbles down over me, a tower falling. It reminds me of a card I saw a long time ago. A pair of cards. A tower and a fool. "You kept him alive. So maybe you're not the most dishonorable man."

"If I'm not the worst man you've ever met, then I'll be shocked." Hades eyes catch the light. Less of him is in shadow now. "I can't imagine Demeter paraded you around the city. Or even let you off the grounds." He laughs, the sound low and rich. "And now look at you."

I don't want to look at myself—I want him to look at me. And he is. Be careful what you wish for, Persephone. He's watching now. The ghost of his fingers pushes into me, again and again. I'm swimming up from a great depth.

"I've had problems, too. Complicated ones."

He narrows his eyes and steeples his fingers in front of his chin. "Eavesdropping is a bad habit. I should train that out of you."

I pull the blanket tighter, but I lean toward him all the same. "How would you do that?"

"It's very simple." The light plays in his eyes, highlighting the blue. "A system of rewards and punishments."

"Like an animal?" What am I saying? Someone else has taken over my body and is now having this conversation like I can't still feel him touching me, even now. "Like how you'd train a dog, or a horse?"

"Are you a dog or a horse, Persephone?"

"No." The room takes on a bizarre hue and I blink it away. "Why is the light so weird in here? You've never explained that." I shouldn't say anything else. "Does it have to do with your dog?"

Hades stays silent for a long moment. He leans forward in his chair, his suit moving with him. I can't stop looking at his arms. His biceps. His strong hands. His fingers.

"You didn't come here to ask me about the light in the room. Or about Conor. Neither of which is your business."

I did, in a way. I came here to ask him everything. Or I came here because it's the middle of the night and something about the late hour has torn down a barrier that was between us. At least I'm pretending that it has. Believing that it has. Am I really so simple that a man's hands on me are all it takes to bind me to him in a way that even my name signed in ink couldn't do? I'm electric, with pulses of energy seeking him with every heartbeat. I want to get closer.

"There's something else I want to know." I lick my lips. Hades' eyes fall to the movement, and when he looks back up at me he's changed again. As if another veil has been stripped away. Something about his eyes. There's something with his eyes. "I wanted to ask you something. Now that you're back."

"There's nothing I need to tell you."

"There is something I need to know." The blanket is soft and insubstantial under my hands, but I gather it up anyway and move to the edge of my seat. The leather is cool against my bare thighs. "I need to know when you're going to fuck me."

For the first time, I've caught him by surprise. The momentary shock is here and gone again. He threads his hands behind his head.

"Why would you think I'd bother fucking you?"

"Don't say that." The numb, dreamlike feeling has spread across my entire face and over my shoulders. What's the worst that happens—he kills me? Some twisted part of me would probably like that, too. "I know you want to. Why haven't you done it yet?"

His eyes—something about his eyes. They're blue, aren't they? But in this light, and with those words hanging in the air between us, they look almost black. There's hardly any color. A shiver runs down my spine.

"I want to know why you haven't done it yet."

"Come here."

There's no point in hesitating. Once I'm on my feet he motions for me to drop the blanket. Suddenly, passionately, I want to keep it wrapped around me —but I know the game he plays. He'll only take it off himself. So I let it fall to the floor and go and stand next to his chair.

It's a massive thing, built for him like everything else in this place has been, with no arms. Hades has created space between him and the desk. Just enough space for me. We look at other in the weird, impossible light.

"Bend over my lap."

I suck in a breath, loud in the quiet of the room. My nerves, numbed by what happened before, rear back to life with a thousand sparkling cuts. Needles all over my skin have me instantly, totally awake.

Hades clicks his tongue. "Still so slow to obey."

He shoves me gracelessly over his lap, legs splayed open, gasping like I'm coming up from deep water. A flash of pain, lace raw on my skin—he's torn off my panties. Then his hand, searching between my legs. Stroking. I'm a little sore from earlier and I flinch away without meaning to. He presses his other hand down at the small of my back, pinning me.

"Here's your answer. Is this what you wanted?"

"I—" I'm struggling for air, for anything. My hips rock uselessly against his legs. I can't stop. I can't stop, and it's so embarrassing, so awful, that another wave of tears comes. Yes, yes, *yes.* "No. I can't want this."

Hades laughs. "But it is. You're wet." His tone lifts to a wondering register. "You're so fucking wet, that if I—" He doesn't bother to describe what he's going to do. He only shoves his fingers back inside, roughly, without warning, without waiting. "You want this. In fact..." He leans even closer so that his breath brushes my ear. "You need this. And I love watching you cry and squirm and beg for it."

"I'm not begging."

"Not yet."

"I thought—" It's difficult, thinking, with the slow thrust of his fingers in and out, in and out, so casual. Almost as if he doesn't know he's doing it. But he does know. "I thought you wanted to hurt me."

"Hurt you?" A note of surprise in his voice. "I would never hurt you." He pushes his fingers in deeper. Too deep. Fresh tears. "Does this feel like pain?"

This is, without question, the realest thing he's ever said to me. The words shimmer in the air, behind my eyelids, through the tears. "It's more complicated than that."

"Because you want it so much." He's fucking me with his fingers, but his voice betrays none of it. "It's dangerous for me to give you what you want."

The sensation builds until it's too much. His fingers. His lap. His office, the furniture looming around me as much as he is. His other hand on the small of my back. He's so big. He's so strong. It's a breathless, needy, desperate hum at the core of me and it's too much. It's too much. It makes me come again. This orgasm is raw, almost painful, a thousand sunburns all concentrated into a bomb. From far away I can hear him coaxing me, surprisingly gentle.

That's it. That's it. Yes.

And then—then—I feel myself twisting, my own body moving, like I'm a puppet on strings. Twisting in his lap. Pushing myself up. Throwing my arms around his neck and kissing him.

It's a deep, vicious kiss, his hand on the back of my neck and the other braced against my hip. I'm straddling him. I don't even know how I got here. But the most tender parts of me, bruised from his fingers, brush against the fabric of his suit. The orgasm peaks and fades. He tastes like snow and fire and the burn of some searing alcohol I can't begin to name. My heart is ready to fly out of my chest. My heart's ready to explode.

Before it's done, before I've managed to reinhabit my body, he pushes me off his lap. I catch the edge of the desk and force myself upright, trembling. By the time I'm on my feet he's standing. Backing up. Eyes blazing. He was telling the truth—there is something about me that's dangerous to him. It takes my breath away, or it gives my breath back—I can't tell. He puts a fist to his mouth, breathing hard. I've done something to him. All this time, he's done things to me, and now I've done something to him.

"Get out."

I open my mouth to argue but Hades raises a hand and points behind me.

"Get. Out."

There's no arguing now.

I turn and go, feeling his eyes on me every step of the way.

19

PERSEPHONE

No door wakes me up in the morning—no swish of Lillian's skirts, no footsteps in the hall, nothing. I swim in a deep and dreamless sleep for a long time and wake up slowly, muscles aching, almost naked. It takes quite a bit of stretching before I feel like climbing out of the bed.

I was wrong about the tray. A silver tray balances neatly on the table next to what I've come to think of as my reading chair. And that's not all—a new robe, pure white, hangs over the back of the chair. What's going on? I shrug it over my shoulders and slip into the seat. I've been sleeping forever, and I'm starving. What happened yesterday laps at my mind like an endless series of waves on sand.

I have to stop thinking of it like that—as what happened, as the thing that happened, as what Hades did. Because what he did was make me come. Three times. A sick, twisted, horrible intense pleasure. Words that shouldn't belong in the same sentence, but there they are.

It's dangerous for me to give you what you want.

What did that mean? I have the sense that there's more to this, something I'm missing. But when I look at it directly, it disappears. It's like a ghost in the night that disintegrates at the first sign of the bathroom light. I rub both hands over my face and look over my breakfast.

I was wrong about the breakfast.

Three plates. One with a slim slice of chocolate cake. One with a fan of strawberries soaked in sugar. One with a cloudlike pastry drizzled with chocolate. Two small pitchers of cream. A mug of coffee, black. A jewelry box. A note.

These are not the normal trappings of breakfast, even here.

A jewelry box?

Note first.

I've never seen his handwriting before but I recognize it instantly—flawless, masculine, taking up every available inch of the small slip of paper.

I've instructed Lillian not to wake you this morning in light of our activities yesterday. You haven't been eating enough, so I had the kitchen replace your meal for the morning. Do better, Persephone. I won't have my property self-destruct. You'd be useless to me then.

—L.H.

He's left a postscript underneath.

The jewelry box is for you.

The note falls from my trembling fingers. A gift? I don't even know what to think of that. I'd been thinking that yesterday was a nightmare and last night was a continuation of a bad dream gone wrong, but now...

I can't make myself wait. The velvet box feels new in my hands. Too light for what it is. It's wide and flat and when I lift the lid the box ceases to matter at all. Because inside is the most beautiful necklace I've ever seen. Wait—two necklaces. Two diamond necklaces. I whip around to make sure nobody's watching. I've never had a necklace like this. I've never had anything like this. Flower crowns and poppy jewelry are all I've ever worn.

The first one reminds me of a lace collar, only the lace has been woven from diamonds. I can picture exactly how it would look if I wore it. Heat tumbles over my cheeks. It's ostentatious, and I bet it's nothing to Hades. I saw his factory yesterday. He could have a million of these if he wanted.

And the second...

The second brings tears to my eyes.

It's a simple chain, platinum maybe, and at the end dangles a delicate disk the size of my fingertip. Etched into the disc is a single poppy. I skim my finger over the tiny raised chips of diamonds and rubies that make up the flower's stem and petals, and memories come crashing in. Sprinting across open fields, barefoot and laughing in the sun. A basket of flowers dangling from my hand. The sweetness of not knowing about the fence, or the train, or the world outside.

This is the one I want to wear, immediately. When I lift the backing from the box to take it out, another note flutters to the floor at my feet.

One for special occasions. The other to remind you where you belong.

It's easy to see which one is which. I put it on, and the slim coin dangles between my breasts while I eat a miniature assortment of some of my favorite foods.

While I shower, working the shampoo through my hair inch by inch and slicking conditioner through every curl.

While I tilt my head beneath the most expensive, quietest hair dryer I have ever seen.

While I hunt through the closet for something not quite as exposing as the rack of white nightgowns Hades has apparently chosen for me, and which I've been wearing since I got here.

In one corner of the closet I find a collection of slim dresses, slightly longer—they hit above the knee, though the fabric borders on sheer, just like the nightgowns. There's no hiding what I'm wearing—or not wearing—underneath. I'm not sure why I didn't see the knee-length caftan at first —it's the only thing in here with any color. A shock of red, like blood. My eyes must have skipped over it, or else it's new from when I went into the shower.

It's perfect.

Sheer, like everything else—light, like everything else. A strong breeze could take it away. But the red color makes me feel…new.

"Persephone?"

Lillian stands partway in the door to the oversized walk-in closet, frowning, dark eyes on me. Something isn't right. In the mirror I watch as she flicks her eyes back in the direction she came, lips pressed into a hard line.

"Is everything all right?"

"There are things you've asked me about." I turn away from the mirror and find her expression transformed. What was I seeing in the reflection? She's not worried, she's determined. Very, very determined. Her dark eyes burn with it. "I got some answers. Come with me."

She doesn't have to say the rest—that only following her, right now, will give me access to the things I want to know. So I do it, stopping only to slip on a pair of white ballet flats. At the door Lillian turns back and murmurs, "Mr. Hades is in his main office. We don't have to worry about passing him in the hall."

I don't know how she could possibly know that for sure, but my curiosity has been piqued. More than piqued. It's been grabbed by the throat and dragged out of me. Frankly, it interrupted my daydreams. But it makes my heart beat faster. Every change in the air on the way out of Hades' private rooms is razor-sharp against my skin.

Long before we get to the rotunda, Lillian stops abruptly by an alcove in the wall. It's nothing—there's no door, just a blank wall. Maybe she's lost it. Maybe I'm following a woman on a fool's errand that will only make things worse for me. I need them to get better, not worse. I'm just not sure what better actually means in this scenario.

She steps up to the wall and presses her hand at a place that looks the same as the rest of the wall. A crack appears. A door slides open. Lillian steps through. Looks back.

"Persephone, hurry."

Secret passageways. Of course he has secret passageways. This isn't just a mansion, and it's not just a factory—it's a fortress. All fortresses are built for secrets.

I'm a secret.

A secret who follows Lillian into the narrowest hallway I've yet to see on the mountain. The door slides shut behind us, amplifying the sound in the hall. It's a muffled quiet, except for our breathing.

"We'll have to move quickly." Lillian turns her head so I can hear her, but she never slows down for an instant. "It's best if we can get back before Mr. Hades decides to leave his office. There should be enough time, but..."

Enough time for what? I don't dare ask. That gnawing need to *know, know, know* expands until my lungs could burst with it. If I let it out into the passageway it'll take down the whole mountain.

It gets narrower the farther we go, tilting down, almost like the passageway is herding us. My heart beats its fists against my ribs. If I've made a mistake in trusting her, it could be a long time before anyone finds me. It could be a very long time. And I have unfinished business. That's an accurate way to describe yesterday and last night. Unfinished business. That kiss—that kiss wasn't finished. I don't know what possessed me, but I want to know.

I'm about to grab Lillian by the elbow and tell her to take me back, right now, when we come up against another flat wall. This side has a notch in the rock at about waist level. She puts her fingers in it and tugs. The door comes open. On the other side is a hallway, pitch dark—no. Not pitch dark. Lit by...flames? Faint flames.

"What is this?" The question sneaks out before I can stop it. "Lillian, where are we?"

Then a form fills the doorframe and for a horrible sickening second I think it's Hades. He caught us. My heart leaps up into my throat. This would deserve a good punishment. I wouldn't be able to argue with him. He'd pin me down and—

"Persephone."

It's not his voice. And now that I look, it's not his body, either; the person in shadow is too tall and thin, almost gaunt. But his green eyes haven't changed.

"Decker. Oh, my god, Deck."

Lillian flattens herself against the wall just in time

for Decker to barrel through the passageway and close me in his arms. He curses gently against the top of my head.

"It all went so wrong." His voice is muffled by the air and the space and his arms around me. "So wrong. It wasn't supposed to go that way." He pushes me back to look at me. "And now he's done things to you." Decker's eyes search mine, a hard set to his mouth. "They made me watch."

"I know. I'm sorry, Deck. That was probably my fault."

He takes my face in his hands and I wait to feel the flood of relief that I...should be feeling. Right now. It should be cascading over me with all the strength of every waterfall on the face of the planet. Decker is alive, even after yesterday. He managed to keep himself alive after witnessing what he witnessed. But that potent relief doesn't materialize.

"How could it have been your fault?" He whispers the words and I'm stricken with the fear that he might try to kiss me. Fear. Real enough to make the hairs on my arms stand on end. I don't want him to kiss me. If he kisses me, I don't know what will happen. Hades might taste it on me. He might feel it on me. "None of this is your fault." He frowns, just a little, guilt like heat lightning in his eyes. There. Gone. In less than a blink, it's gone. Did I imagine it? Decker screws up his mouth and strokes my cheeks with his thumbs. "He's a piece of shit." Thunder in his voice, a tremor in his hands. "That guy—he's pure evil."

He's not.

That's what comes to mind, and to the tip of my tongue. He's not. The necklace Hades left me this morning sits lightly over my collarbone, the chain whispering on my skin. He knew about the poppies, somehow. Or he guessed that they mean something to me and always have. And the food—the *food.*

"I'm all right," I say instead.

"There's no fucking way you could be. The things he's doing to you—they'll make you—" Decker shakes his head. He can't finish. "Look, I don't have much time before I have to get back. You probably have to get back, too. But it's okay, Persephone."

"I was so worried." Worried he'd be dead. Worried that it would be my fault. Now that he's standing in front of me, I should feel relieved but I'm not. I'm more on edge than I've been since we arrived at the mountain. I rise up on tiptoe, trying to ease myself away from the sensation. It's a wild anxiety that can only be soothed by going back to my own room.

"I'm fine." A glint comes into his eyes. "Better than fine now."

"You have to leave, though. If Hades catches you—"

"Forget that asshole." Now a smile spreads across his face. "You don't understand—we're getting out of here. We're getting out of this hellhole."

"We have to leave, Persephone." Lillian's voice is low, urgent.

"I can't leave." What the hell does Decker *mean*?

"I have a way to get us on the train." He glances back over his shoulder at the open door. "Just trust me. I'll send someone to get you. Okay? Be ready." Decker looks me up and down. "Try to wear something better for traveling, but if you can't, then I won't complain."

His smile is the same smile from back at the farm, big and genuine and handsome. He looks exactly the same. He even smells the same, faintly dusty and warm.

Something is different. Me. I'm different.

"What happens after the train? He won't just let me go."

"You let me worry about that. I've got it figured out. Five days. A week, tops. Then we're gone, and you never have to see him again. Soon. Got it?"

Soon I'll be on the train, heading toward New York City. It's where I always wanted to go. That's my dream. How can I even hesitate? Except there's dread in my stomach. I signed that contract, fully intending to follow through. Fully intending to trade my own freedom for Decker's life. Except now he's here offering me escape.

It's more than that, though. I've been on this mountain for minutes, hours, days—and it's enough to make me feel safe. To make this feel almost like home. It's a crazy idea. I'm not safe with Hades, no matter how many orgasms he gives me.

And even if I was, I'll never find freedom locked up in my room here.

"Soon," I say, ignoring the knot in my stomach.

In the far distance a whistle sounds and Decker lets go of my face. "Be ready."

"I'll be waiting."

His face softens, lights up. He blows me a kiss.

Lillian nods. "We have to get back to the room."

Decker stops one final time, his dirt-stained hand on the door panel. He looks back, and his face is almost completely in shadow. "It's almost over, Persephone."

20

HADES

DEMETER IS OUT OF CONTROL.

Her daughter has barely been gone a week, and the reports come in fast and furious. She's stormed into the city, looking for Zeus. She's hired a man to search the city underground for her.

She's lighting her fields on fire, one by one.

"Oliver. Tell me you're fucking kidding. Tell me this is one of your jokes."

Oliver shifts his weight from foot to foot, hands in his pockets. He'd rather not be out in the relative openness of the office. He's a man who'd rather cling to the shadows. That's where all the real work gets done.

"I don't tell jokes."

"Then tell me which field she started with." It's the information that means the most to me now. I *have* to know. Lives depend on it, mine included.

He shakes his head.

"Find out."

Oliver leaves without another word. I wait until he's gone and then leave the office, too. Silence expands around me as I go. It's earlier than I'd normally leave, but fuck—the news has made me want to tear down all the glass just to hear it shatter.

Fucking Demeter. There was once a time I could admire how ruthless she is, but if she thinks this is the way to smoke out who has Persephone?

She's probably fucking right.

Because as much as Demeter likes to pretend that she's in the bridal business, that's only a front. It's always been a front. Her real business is far more lucrative and far more dangerous than bouquets wrapped in white ribbon. And if she's become so unhinged that she's burning her business to the ground to force someone's hand…

To force *my* hand.

I can see it now—Demeter with lighter fluid in the dry evening of early summer. Demeter lowering a match to the ground. Flames swallowing the fields whole.

The woman is going to kill me. She'll kill me, and then what will happen to Persephone? If I'm dead, this place will riot. They'll come for Persephone first. They'll come for Demeter second. We'll all end up under the ground, but it'll be me first. And then who will protect Persephone? No one.

My skin feels too tight, my mood too thunderous to be contained in this body. I have been containing it for years. I have been denying myself for years. I have kept everything so close to my chest that my biggest secret is a throbbing dagger through my heart. I can't take a single fucking step without feeling it there, lodged in deep. Not a single step. Conor shoves against my legs, hard. He wants me the fuck out of here—away from the factory's bright lights. Not even the tinted windows of my office can mitigate them fully.

I have to clear my head.

The easiest way, the path of least resistance, would

be to go down to the mines and find some criminal fucker who's been sentenced here as a cheap alternative to a prison sentence and squeeze the life out of him. But the easiest way won't be enough. Not tonight. Not when Demeter's fields burn and Oliver takes the train at top speed to see whether it's my life or someone else's that's rising into the sky like so much ash.

I don't know that I've gone to find her until I'm pushing open the door to Persephone's suite. Conor stays to guard the door. He's learned.

The lights are down low, but they're on. No sign of her in the bed. Her dinner tray, with a ruby red pomegranate in a silver dish, sits nearly untouched on a table by the window.

Where the fuck is she?

I don't call her name. She'll learn soon enough that hiding from me like this—it's not a fucking option. She'll pay for this. She will. I strip off my jacket and let it fall to the floor. If I have to search the entire mountain myself to find her, I will. She'd better pray I don't have to search the mountain.

Every sense is jacked up to its maximum sensitivity as I make my way down the narrow hall, shoving open doors as I go. She's not in the bathroom. The shower is dry. She's not in the closet, with all the white nightgowns that double as dresses. I put them in here to embarrass her. It's been worth it to see her face every time I scan a hemline.

For a heart-stopping moment, the library looks empty, too. Rage squeezes at the muscle in the center of my chest until my blood flows backward. Then her foot, curled up at the edge of the overstuffed chair by the fireplace, catches my attention. She's here. My eyes burn, but not from tears. Never from tears. I don't bother to take quiet footsteps on my way to the side table. The lamp in here—I must've missed it.

Persephone doesn't stir at the crack of the switch. She doesn't seem to feel me looming over her, and I breathe in that innocence. She doesn't know how much I need her. She doesn't know. For this one final moment, she doesn't know. She's nothing but flowing fabric and bare ankles, a small heap in the chair with a book held tight to her chest. Asleep in the glow of the fireplace.

I can see echoes of Demeter in her face.

I can see Persephone doing the same thing, laughing as she burns down the world.

My pulse pounds in my ears.

But I make myself wait.

Even now, I make myself wait.

I unbutton my shirt and roll the sleeves up to my elbows. I loosen the top button. I watch her breathing, slow and even.

What does she dream about?

Not this.

"Get up."

Persephone's eyes snap open at the sound of my voice, wide and terrified. The energy in a tight ball at the base of my gut bursts apart, all static and lightning and anger. She doesn't know where she is, and now it's dark. I can see her in the kind of stark detail that makes her panting fucking mouth-watering.

"Does get up mean keep lying there to you? Get up."

She scrambles to get up, but her arm is asleep or

else I've scared her so badly she can't move. "I'm trying." Her cry reverberates off the glass statue on the top bookshelf. "I'm trying."

"Get. Up."

"Why?"

Her gasp blows apart the very last shred of my restraint. It's been weakened by the drumbeat of my own heart in my ears, by the flames in the fields, and having to touch her sweet body and not fuck her for what seems like an eternity.

I haul her up from the seat by her clothes, the seams ripping in my hands. Straight into the air. Straight up until she's level with my face, her lips opening and closing. "Because I fucking need you," I growl into her mouth, and then I kiss her.

Because I want to.

Because I've waited.

Because last night, when she turned over in my arms and flung herself into me and kissed me like that, it almost killed me.

And I'd rather die this way than any other.

She tastes sweet and clean and soft and the

panicked little noises at the back of her throat drive me wild, then wilder, until there's not much man left at all. Do I pull her into my arms, or does she climb up, her legs wrapped around my waist? Does she cry before I yank her head back by the hair and lick up the length of her neck or is it only after? I bite down on her bottom lip until the moment she starts to scream, and then I pull back. "You didn't eat your dinner."

Persephone is the picture of confusion. "I wasn't hungry"

"Liar." It's nothing to carry her back out to the main room, put her on her feet, and bend her over the tray. "You're starving. You just don't know it."

"I was reading." Her voice shakes. "I meant to come finish it."

"When I tell you to finish something, you do it first, sweetheart, or you'll suffer the consequences."

A shiver rocks her under my hand, electric, and she murmurs something into the pomegranate.

"I can't fucking hear you."

"Please."

Her voice rings like a bell through the room and that's all it takes. I thought I was undone before. That was nothing compared to now. I force her down onto her knees and rip her clothing to shreds. Indiscriminate. It doesn't matter what it is, I want her skin exposed to me now. Her perfect pink nipples are already peaked, her thighs spread—she wants this. Fuck me. She wants it as much as she hates it.

The pomegranate next.

I rip it apart in my hands, the two halves glistening in my palms, and drop most of it back to the table. Persephone's chest heaves with every breath. She has relatively small tits, but they're a nice shape, and they'll be even nicer covered in the juice from the pomegranate. It shears apart easily in my hands.

She doesn't struggle when I take her chin in my hand and tip her head back. She looks up at me with her huge, depthless gaze. Her lips are slightly parted. I work a thumb between her teeth and force them open farther.

"Eat."

It's awkward for her because I make it awkward. I make it mortifying. I make it awful, and it drives me to the very edge of my own sanity. One by one, I lift each piece of the fruit to her lips and make her scrape the seeds out with her teeth. After the second section she tries to lift her hands to wipe the juice away from her chest.

"Put your hands behind your back. Move them again, and I'll put you over my knee and spank you until you can't sit down."

I can see the tremor in her muscles. It's a dead give-away. She thinks about doing it, but I shove her mouth full of the fruit. Again, and again, and again. Until her mouth is full, and then I make her chew. Swallow. Again. Again. Again.

I have to get down on one knee to kiss her, to lick some of the juice out of her mouth. A surge of life hits my blood like the world's best painkiller. The ever-present burn in my eyes subsides, at least for the moment.

This time, I can't stop.

I'm fucking exhausted and I'm wide awake, and reality shears away from what's happening with Persephone. This reality, with her mouth on mine, is the only one that matters.

The floor, the chair, the bed. I can't say how we get to either place, only that it must be me. I'm holding her hands pinned behind her back. I'm kissing her. Scraping my teeth over her nipples. Biting the sensitive skin at the curve of her neck.

I can't stop.

I have to stop.

If I cross that bright line, then everything else that matters is going to burn.

Maybe it already has.

But on the off-chance that it hasn't, I shove her away, back onto the bed. Persephone falls hard, not bothering to put her hands out to catch herself. I'm halfway to the door when she gets herself up.

"Don't go." Her voice is wobbly but clear. "Please, don't go."

"Why not."

"Because I need it."

21

PERSEPHONE

HE STOPS. Turns. Looks.

I am destroyed already. I am nothing but a throbbing bundle of nerves on the verge of an even more drastic destruction. If he leaves me here now, with every sense on edge, on fire, then I'll scream and never stop screaming. I hate him. I need him. I need so many dark and twisted things that I can't even fathom how depraved I've become. His necklace has twisted around and hangs down my back—I can feel it between my shoulder blades.

I am destroyed, and I'm looking at a man on the verge of his own destruction.

I know it without quite knowing it. There's no way I

can know it for sure. I've never met a man like Hades but I *know* him. I've only met a few men in my life, and I've always been ushered quickly away by my mother. There was never time. There was never a chance. Except for Decker. And I never saw him like this—not even when Hades was killing him.

His blue eyes catch every available bit of light, making him look otherworldly, like something out of a dream or a nightmare. It's so beautiful it hurts. He is so flawless it cuts me in some place I didn't know existed. The wanting—the wanting could turn me inside out, all on its own. If I couldn't see him breathing I would think he wasn't a man at all. Something more. Something darker. Something that could consume me.

Something that already has.

"You don't know what you need."

His words hit me like one stone after another, connecting with all my softest places. I get up onto my knees on the bed. I'm already naked. There's nothing else he can take from me, except this.

And is it taking if I'm the one who's giving it?

Power surges through me like I've grabbed an electric fence. I thought I'd never have this feeling, not ever in my life. I thought it would always belong to my mother, and then to Hades. *I thought, I thought, I thought*. All those things are meaningless now. Worthless.

"I do."

Hades hasn't moved. He stands sideways, the long lines of him illuminated by the lamp on my bedside table. His face has never been so open to me before, so readable. Hades, the most powerful man I have ever known, wears the expression of someone who has known incredible pain.

I wait for the door to slam shut between us. For him to turn on his heel and walk away, leaving me here to writhe under the covers all night and into the morning. For the wall he builds every day to close over this new knowledge of him like a prison gate, hiding him from me once and for all.

"You have no fucking idea."

"I want you." My voice falls to a whisper and I clear my throat, desperate to keep talking, desperate to keep him here. "I want this."

"What's *this*, Persephone?" His lip curls, a sneer if I've ever seen one, but I see through it, beneath it. He's trying to rebuild the distance between us. It's too late. I've kissed him and I've tasted him and I need to see this through to the bitter end. "You want me to fuck you like the useless slut that you are?"

My heart absorbs the blow, then rejects it, spitting it out like poison.

"That's not what you really think." A tear slips out of the corner of my eye and I see how it affects him —see his eyes widen, his lips part. He does love it. He needs it, too. "I know it's not."

Hades turns toward me, and once again I'm struck by how big he is. I don't know what kind of fate I'm tempting by fighting with him. Wait—I do know. I'm tempting death itself.

Death in a white dress shirt. Death in pants that hug the muscles of his legs like the fabric was grown while it hung on his body. Death in his eyes—a warning, a promise. Violence, all wrapped up in expensive cloth.

"If I come over there, I will ruin you." This, delivered so lightly I can almost feel his breath on my lips. "I will ruin you. You'll never be the same."

"Then ruin me. Do it. I'm not afraid." I *am* afraid. I've never been more afraid of reaching this moment and what comes after.

His face is a firestorm. "What if I want you to be the same, you little fool? What if I want to keep you exactly as innocent as you are until you go mad from it?"

"I'm almost there." I'm there. I am there *anyway.* No matter how innocent he wants me. Being near him has made me dirty, made me filthy. A dam breaks, bursting. "I can't take it much longer—the waiting. Waiting for you to come back and touch me."

"Don't waste your energy. I'll touch you when I please. I'll bend you over when I please. I'll destroy you when I please."

"But you won't." I eke out the words on a breath. Another crack in his armor, quickly disguised. "Maybe you'll destroy the person I was, but I'm already gone. You can never get that girl back. And *I* don't want to get her back. I want you to finish the job."

"What makes you think I owe you anything?"

"Because I belong to you." My teeth clench and heat spills over my skin. A hundred degrees. A thousand degrees. Hotter. "And I need more."

He's silent. Still.

"It will be the end of you," he says simply. He means it. His face settles into a cautious expression, watching me. "It will be the fucking end."

"We both know you don't care." I deliver this blow like a knife slipped gently through soft flesh. It's what he's been saying to me all along. Hades glances down at his shirt like I've actually stabbed him. When he lifts his head again, his eyes don't just burn. They blaze.

I'm frozen.

This is the moment where everything comes together or everything comes apart, and if he walks away now, I don't think I'll be able to stand it. I think I'll sink into the softest, most comfortable bed I've ever slept in, pull the covers over my head, and die. The anticipation is too much. It's killing me. But he's killing me just as much, by taking me in such small increments. If I'm going to belong to him then he needs to make the final move. He needs to make it now. Otherwise I'll always wonder what would have happened if Decker had walked into a different train car.

Once he does what he's planning to do—and I know he's planning to do it, I saw it in his eyes the first day we met—then all the wondering will stop. I know it will. This is the last mountaintop to scale. This is the last submission. There is nothing else after this.

"You're right, sweetheart." A wicked, twisting smile crosses his face. He reaches for one of the arms of his shirt, shoved up near his elbows. I have never seen forearms like his—not even on men like Decker. Not even from far away. Perversely I want to lick them. Bite them, the way he's bitten me. "I don't care."

It's comforting, in a way—that he says it before he yanks his sleeves down one by one and strips off his shirt to reveal a pristine white undershirt. His clothes are always so clean, even when he's going to choke a man to death.

"You do," I whisper. Too soft for him to hear. He hears it anyway.

And slowly, wearing that smile that twists my stomach into a thousand knots, he shakes his head.

"You've begged so prettily," he comments, the way a person would comment on the weather or the arrival of the mail. "I almost believe, Persephone—I almost believe that you want this."

"I do want this."

Maybe I don't. Maybe I don't want him to fuck me, to ruin me, to destroy me. But what else is there to want, other than to have it over with? What else am I supposed to feel about it? The thudding in my ears, my own heartbeat, never goes away. Not even when I sleep. I am always on edge, even in my dreams. I need this from him, even if I don't exactly want it. Even if I don't know what I'm wanting, no matter how much I insist that I do.

There's another way out of this situation, and it's to become someone else. Someone who is not me. Someone who does not worry about what's going to happen every moment of every day. Someone who has nothing left to lose.

I want it so badly it makes me cry.

All he needs to do is finish the job, that's all. He's taken me this far and to hold back from pushing me off the precipice is more than cruel. It will be the death of me. And some small part of me thinks that Hades, for all his talk, wants me to be alive. What use would I be to him dead? No use. No use at all.

My legs start to tremble, to shake, and I lower myself down onto my heels. He huffs a laugh, and all of the bravado I've built up in the heat of the moment dissolves. I'm on the other side of that doorway. His face has shifted back into the beautiful cruelty he always wears. The cruelty that would allow him to let Decker dangle from his hands. The cruelty that let him push his fingers inside of me in front of everyone on his factory floor. Something about him scared my mother enough that she spent my entire life warning me off of him.

This is it. This look, on his face, right now. Like I'm prey. Like he could dangle me from his hands and watch the life slowly leave me, unblinking, uncaring. But something shifts at the last moment. He wouldn't kill me. He might hurt me. But that's as far as he'll go.

And then he moves.

The way he moves is nothing short of astounding, even in shirtsleeves and his custom slacks. He moves through the world as though he knows every inch of it as intimately as he'd know a lover. As if he's spent hours running his hands over every available surface, memorizing it. A graceful killer.

My body responds while my mind tries frantically to convince me that this is fine, this is what I asked for, this is what I wanted. The tears come first, totally unbidden. Hades stops at the edge of the bed, takes my face roughly in his hand, and pulls me toward him. He licks the salt from the side of my face and leans in close to scrape his teeth across my bottom lip, stinging.

His eyes rake across my face, studying, devouring. Not even Decker has looked at me like this—not once. I mistook the way Decker used to look at me for a hunger that could never be satisfied. Now I'm not sure if anyone but Hades could be that ravenous.

Hades slams a hand down on the table. Does he even hit the switch? I don't know, and it doesn't matter—the light goes off, plunging us into darkness. My eyes adjust while I gasp for air. Moonlight. It streams through the windows on the opposite side of the room, bathing us in white and leaching all the color from the room. It doesn't matter. He's just as menacing, and just as breathtaking, without it.

"You're ruined."

I am.

22

PERSEPHONE

I'M NOT EXPECTING tenderness of any kind.

In fact, I don't want it.

It still takes me by surprise when Hades drags me off the bed and stands my feet on the floor. He kicks them apart and shoves me down over the bed, bent over, exposed. My breath comes fast and hard and hot. He catches one wrist in his hand, then the other. I don't know where the tie comes from, but I feel the slip and slide of it over my wrists. Hades tugs at them, the movement dispassionate.

"Move your wrists."

I can do it, if only a little. Tenderness. Maybe this is just because he doesn't want to cut off circulation in my hands, but the fact that he doesn't want that—it means he feels something. Anything at all. Not that it's part of the deal. His emotions are not on the table. They have never been on the table.

He stands up behind me and caresses my ass with one wide palm. I've almost let myself relax into the sensation when he spanks me, once, sharply. I lurch up from the bed, crying out, and he pushes me back down like I'm nothing. Spanks me again.

"I could do this all night."

He could—I believe him. I don't know what I'm being punished for but it could be any number of things. Falling asleep. Keeping him waiting. Sneaking away to meet Decker. He could know about all of that. I'd deserve it. But the more he spanks me, the more I want it. A stinging heat spreads across my backside. Ten or fifteen later—I've lost count in the haze—he shoves his fingers between my legs.

"What did I do?" I've been crying again, without knowing it. And I know I didn't do anything. I know this is punishment for the sake of punishment. I also know that my questions wind him up. Coil him tight. I keep my feet firmly planted on the floor even as my thighs tremble. "Why are you doing this?"

It's a plaintive question and my voice sounds small, even to me.

"So it's easier to fuck you." He adds a few more for good measure and I gasp every time. "This is your favorite thing, you twisted little slut."

"Only for you—only when you—"

"I've done things to you that made you so fucking wet you could hardly stand up straight. But I'll give you this one, Persephone. You waited quite a while to beg me to fuck you. You're an angel."

Angel sounds worse than slut. *Angel* sounds like a woman who wears only white and sleeps with her hands above the covers, never getting pleasure out of anything. *Angel* sounds like the endgame. You can't be an angel and be anything else. I want him to take my wings.

"Now shut your mouth."

He spanks me to remind me, until my ass burns. It must be red. He can't see how red it is, not in the moonlight, and that's one saving grace. Hades rubs at my sore flesh absently. Out of the corner of my eye I can see him watching me.

"Those tears." He sucks in a breath. "Those, more than anything, make me want to keep you just how you are."

He said to shut my mouth but I can't help myself. "Then you're going to keep me?"

Hades pushes thick fingers into me, as deep as he can, before he answers. "You'd rather die than belong to me."

"No." One shuddering breath, then another. "I'm alive."

He curls his fingers, and I am ended.

I don't know what he's touched or where, but he does it again and brings down all the lightning the world has ever seen in one massive bolt at the deep center of me. I can feel myself clenching on the fingers, tighter and tighter. He does it again. Again. Again. I lose count of how many times I jerk and come because of him. They blur together, one ending, another beginning, peaking constantly until the tears on my cheeks are from being completely overloaded by his hands. By his fingers.

"There's more than one way to punish a woman," he says. Or at least I think he says it. It could be my own brain finally losing its grip on reality. "More than this, Persephone."

I brace for another spanking, but instead I hear a sound I can't immediately place.

Clothes, hitting the floor.

I'm not wearing any more clothes.

I'm bent over the edge of the bed, panting and quaking and only upright by the grace of Hades himself.

Those have to be his clothes.

I've had too much to turn my head, though I want to see him.

I want to see him, but I don't need to see him. All I need to do is feel him. He touches me, making the first contact. The air around us ignites. He slides his palms down my back, traces a path down my spine. Then he braces them against my hips.

"I'm going to hold you still while I take you." Like he's commenting on the weather. "You weren't hoping for someone to kiss you and wipe away your tears, were you?"

I shake my head no. I wish he would just do it. I wish he would take us to the other side of whatever this is. Maybe that's crazy. Maybe it's not something I should ever want, and it makes me just as bad as he is. But I've never killed anyone. I've only begged a killer to do depraved things to my body. I don't know what that makes me, and right now I don't care.

"Good."

Hades shifts behind me, and I can't for the life of me figure out what he's going to do. It doesn't feel like being fucked, which I'm assuming has something to do with a dick, not—

Not a tongue.

Not a tongue pressing possessively against me.

Licking. Long, broad strokes. My flesh is already swollen and wanting and his tongue on it sets me on fire as much as his hands do, spreading me even wider. I didn't think it was possible.

It's possible.

He licks and nips in endless strokes that push wave after wave of pleasure over me. Pleasure so intense it aches and stings. A pleasure to meet the pain of his hand on my ass before. I hate him for it. I need him for it. Hate and need hold each other with a tight grip. They show no signs of letting go.

How can he be the one to do this to me? How can I want it so much? The questions loop around and around until they finally drown themselves in pleasure. In pleasure, there are no questions. There are only answers. And the answer is an earth-shattering orgasm that has me bucking against the tie around my wrist. I would be rocking into the side of the bed, only Hades' hands on my waist pin me in place. Just like he promised.

He pushes his tongue inside me, farther than I thought it could go, then pulls back. I howl against the bedding. It's awful, it's awful. He's awful for stopping. I wanted more, and he could have given it to me.

But he was only preparing me for what's to come.

Which is the thickness of him pressing harshly against my opening. Which is his hands, pressing tight against my hips, tight enough to bruise. Which is *say goodbye, sweetheart.* I don't get the words to wish the old me farewell before he takes me with one single, relentless thrust.

It tears through me, pain screaming between my legs—or maybe that's me screaming. He's torn something, he's hurt something, and I know that intellectually that's what's supposed to happen, that's what I asked him to do, but I didn't know it would feel like this. I didn't know he would feel so huge. There's not enough room. He can't fit, but he makes himself fit. He's stretching me too far. I'll never be able to take it all.

But I don't have a choice.

I don't want a choice.

He pulls out and drives back inside, inch by inch, and I feel everything. Every ridge, every iron millimeter. My body convulses around him in something like an orgasm, only wretched and tear-filled and bad. It's bad, to have this happen to me.

And it's so, so good.

I don't know that at first—all I feel is the pain. Hades doesn't stop for an instant. He doesn't let up for a single moment. He fucks me hard, like he has always owned me. Like this isn't special—it's just something he does. It's not special. It's the end of the world.

Thank god, it's the end of the world.

Blood and pleasure mix around him and slowly, gradually, I become aware that it doesn't feel quite so sharp and cutting anymore. He might fit. He does fit. It's a near thing. He takes all the available space, he fills me to the hilt, but I'm handling it. I'm managing it.

I'm more than managing it.

I discover that I'm murmuring pleas instead of crying, rocking back against his hands since I can't move enough to get more of him into me. I'm moving with him. There is no other way to move. He sets the rhythm, he chooses the thrust, he is in control of everything.

It sets me free.

He's a vicious lover, never seeming to care what I need. Or maybe he did care, and I got what I was going to get at the beginning. Or maybe he knows me better than I know myself. Because the more he fucks me the tighter the pleasure winds until finally he's driving into me so hard I can't catch my breath, holding me hard enough to bruise, and I come harder than I ever thought possible.

It shouldn't be possible. It's blinding, heart-stopping, unearthly. Who's screaming? Me, or someone else? It doesn't matter. The spiral twists and releases again. I'm dimly aware of him working harder. Faster. And there's a deep, final thrust, a noise from somewhere in the back of his throat, and something hot spilling into me.

Opening my eyes seems out of the question.

After a long time, or maybe only a few minutes, Hades works himself out of me. I'm left knock-kneed and panting on the bed. I still don't open my eyes. I'm not going to open them. The tie slides off my wrists, and he moves on to the bed and rolls one wrist, then the other, making sure move them. At some point he picks me up. Water runs in the bathroom, steam kissing my face. I discover for the first time that there's a ledge in the shower wide enough for a man to sit on with a woman in his lap.

Soap on a washcloth. His hair, wet in the shower. Blue eyes carved from the sky tracing every available path along by body, wiping away the sweat and the blood and all the evidence that nothing is the same now. His hands in my hair, working in the shampoo and working it back out again. The sweet scent of conditioner.

A towel so soft I could cry, rubbed in gentle circles over every aching inch of me. He wraps another towel around my hair, leaving it on long enough to draw out most of the moisture.

Gathers me into his lap.

Runs a comb through the tangles.

It's a process, with hair like mine, but he sees it through.

I keep my eyes closed.

If I open them, he'll disappear—I know it. Or I will discover that all of this has brought me back where I started. And I don't want to go back there. I never want to go back. There's nothing there for me now—now that I have this.

Clothes—another white dress, a nightgown, slipped over my head. The sway of his body on the way back to the bedroom. He peels back the blankets and deposits me between cool sheets. Tugs up the blankets.

A kiss whispers against my forehead. That—that's a bridge too far for Hades. It must be a hallucination.

Now I do try to open my eyes. I should ask him. I should ask him whether the kiss was real. Whether any of this was real. But I've kept them closed too long, and now I'm drifting.

Is he even here?

I try to get my lips to form the words, but they won't cooperate. My only choice is to sink down into the pillow and drift.

There's something else I should do. What is it? It seemed so important, all this time. Something about a secret passageway and a plan. A way back to my old life. The details are not forthcoming. They don't seem to matter much anymore. Not enough to convince me to wake up and shake off the blankets. I consider it for what seems like several years, but in the end, I can't remember what I was considering in the first place.

I turn over once, my cheek making contact with the other side of the pillow, and I'm lost to the world.

23

PERSEPHONE

I'M WALKING the length of an open field, weaving between the flowers, the grass tickling my bare feet. My basket hangs from one hand. Its balance is perfect. I've arranged the small weights of the flowers so that the basket swings along with every step, catching the breeze. Summer sun. I've always loved the summer sun. It's warm on my face, on my shoulders. The hem of my dress whispers along my ankles, gauzy and clean. No one watches me.

There's no rush, is there? There's never been any rush. I could spend all day crossing this field, if I wanted. I have plans to eat an apple once I get to the other side. A bright red apple, sweet and fresh. A perfect globe. Grown for me. I can see for miles. No fences cut me off from the world, but I don't need a fence. I'm perfectly content to walk back home when I'm finished with my task.

A hand tugs at my shoulder.

"Mmm, no." I shake it off, turning my head to smile at whoever is there. One of the companions my mother hires from the city when she thinks I'm too lonely, maybe. A girl—a young woman. Always a woman. She'll walk with me as long as I want. She'll keep me in sight. It doesn't bother me. "I'm not finished yet."

A drop of water hits the sky and makes the blue ripple all through fluffy white clouds. That shouldn't be happening, probably. I've never seen the sky do that before.

This time, the hand on my shoulder is rougher. More demanding.

"Stop." I brush it away and spin around to confront whoever is there.

The field is empty.

It's not just empty here, it's empty as far as I can see. There is no house. There are no trees. There aren't any flowers.

They grab my shoulder again and shake.

"Stop," I shout, whirling around. They were behind me. There has to be someone there, digging their fingers into my dress and yanking, harder and harder. "What do you want? *What do you want*?"

The dream shifts, and then I'm standing in front of the New York Public Library. The lions watch me with judgment on their stone faces. "You don't belong here," one of them says. The other nods his agreement.

The fabric of my dress seems to pull me up toward the sky and beyond, outside the atmosphere and into the blackness of space. My vision shuts down. It's too dark. I fumble for the covers and pull them up against my shoulder. Pull them tight. I'm tired. I'm too tired to understand what's happening, one foot firmly planted in this dream world.

"Persephone. Persephone, it's time to go."

The voice registers one word at a time, all of them distorted at first and finally clear. My eyes are tiny sandbags. I force one open, then the other. Lillian hovers above me, face almost invisible in the dark.

What is she doing here?

She shakes me again, as if my open eyes aren't a sign of being awake. "Persephone, get up. We have to go. He's waiting."

It must be Hades. There can be no other explanation. I'm so exhausted that I don't open my mouth to ask. No one else would make her worry like this. He hasn't been in the habit of waking me up at night, but maybe he needs more from me. I need more from him. It beats in me like my own heart, an echoed beat a moment out of time so I can always, always hear it.

I make a sound that's meant to be *okay* but is more of an acquiescent mumble. It's the middle of the night. Which night, I don't know. I could have been sleeping for a full day. Two days, even. That's how tired I am. It takes everything I have to swing my legs to the edge of the bed and wriggle out. Lillian kneels down and lines up a pair of shoes on the floor. Shoes? I should be wearing slippers. There's no way I'm walking that far. But they're soft shoes, and comfortable, so I close my eyes and let her tie them up.

"Good," she murmurs. "Good." While I'm still sitting on the edge of the bed, she tugs something around my shoulders and helps me get my arms into the holes. A robe, but thicker. Almost a coat. It has a row of buttons down the front but she doesn't button them. Instead she takes my hand and tugs me to standing. "This way," she coaxes. "He's waiting. We don't have much time."

Hades' private rooms are dark, but I don't need to see much to follow Lillian. She keeps her hand on mine, at times curving her arm around my waist. God, I'm tired. I never thought I could be this tired. I never thought that I could ever be so at peace here in this mountain prison. It doesn't seem much like a prison now. I haven't sorted that out yet. In order to do that, I'll need several hours curled up in the library. The book doesn't matter much. It only needs to be a story that will hold my attention while my mind works in the background. No wonder my mother never let me keep many books. She must have known I'd figure out a way to escape earlier on.

I'm still thinking about sitting in the chair and the weight of a hardcover book in my lap when we go out into the hallway. I let out a little laugh. My voice sounds rough, like I've been up all night, though I know I've been sleeping deeply enough to dream. Is this a dream?

Lillian glances at me. "What is it?"

"His office." I shake my head and laugh again. "It makes so much sense."

She presses her lips together but doesn't say anything else. That's fine. It's the middle of the night, after all. Someone had to wake her up in order to come get me. Hades could have fetched me himself, if that's what he wanted, but who am I to judge what he does? I can't even pay that close of attention just now. Soon we'll be at his office, and then I'll find out what he wants. Lillian can go back to her bed.

"I'm hurrying," I tell her, feeling strange. "I'm hurrying as fast as I can."

"You'll have to go a little faster." She looks around behind her. Behind her? If we're headed toward Hades, there's nobody behind her now. "But not for long."

Exhaustion descends again, making my eyelids feel a thousand times heavier. We turn down one hall, then another. The big circular rotunda at the center of the house is empty. Our footsteps echo against the high ceiling and bounce back down to us. I'm intimately aware of the sound and how it feels hitting my skin. Can a person feel vibrations like that, just from footsteps? It's an interesting question. I bet Lillian doesn't want to talk about it right now. That's okay. There will be plenty of time to talk later.

It's not until we're going down the wide stairs toward the train platform that I open my eyes all the way, blinking hard to try to clear the sleep from them.

The train idles on the tracks, massive engine turning over.

That familiar heat in my cheeks comes back full force, the combination of embarrassment and anticipation. Hades is taking me to the New York Public Library. He must know that I want to go there, and he's taking me there in the middle of the night. I reach up and rub the coin necklace between my fingers. We'll have to fly, or at least drive, once we get back to the city. That sends a thrill down to the tips of my toes. My mother relied on the train for everything. We've never owned a car. The thought of him behind the wheel...god, I don't know much about driving, but I'd like to watch him do it.

Lillian takes one look at the train, hooks her arm through mine, and starts to run.

"What are you doing?"

"The train is leaving," she shouts. "You have to be on it. Run, Persephone. *Now.*"

In that moment, the grass prickly and slick under my feet, I snap fully awake. This isn't some romantic trip across the state line to the library. This is escape.

This is my only chance at freedom.

We run, awkward and stumbling, down the side of the platform. It doesn't make any sense, but I'm too busy trying to catch my breath to figure anything out. Hades doesn't ride in a car at the back of the train—he just doesn't. And I've been mistaken about the size of the platform. It narrows, heading back along the tracks, the wood getting more worn as we go. Up ahead, shadows move in and out of sight. Not shadows—men. They're loading a train car. A tone sounds, a one-two melody.

"It's leaving," Lillian cries. "Go."

She pushes me forward at the same time the activity ahead increases. They're loading the last few crates.

I keep going until I'm level with the men and then—

Decker runs out, a crate in his arms. He hops up onto the train car and sets it down, then jumps back out.

He's not even looking at me. He looks over my head, back toward the tunnel. His eyes go wide. "No fucking way."

Something black and metal appears from the waistband of his pants. I have just enough time to turn—to see Conor barreling toward us, coming at top speed. My breath stops short.

"No!"

My shout is drowned out by the gunshot.

The bullet is close. *So* close. But it doesn't hit me—it goes past, faster than I can see, and Conor goes down hard. He howls, wounded, angry, the howl becoming a desperate whine. My heart shatters and my ears ring, and everything is coming apart. Where did he get a *gun*?

"Persephone, *now*."

He reaches for my hand and pulls me onto the very

last train car. It's empty aside for the crates. Decker slams the door shut behind us and throws down a simple wooden bar over the door. It's like something out of the past. It *is* something out of the past. I'm sure of it.

He bows his head.

He's...praying.

The train starts forward, slow for only a breathless moment, and then it picks up speed, whisking us out of the mountain. The moment we're out under the starry skies, Decker rushes to the window.

"Yes." His voice is full of triumph. "We made it." He comes back to me and looks me up and down. "We both made it. Yes. You're out, Persephone, and I killed that fucking dog." Decker's eyes shine with a strange light. He looks...unhinged. For the first time since I've met him, I'm afraid of him. Which doesn't make any sense at all. Decker is here to save me. He sits down heavily on one of the crates and rubs his hands over his face. "Sit down, okay? Relax. We'll be there soon. And then...then it'll all be over."

The reality of this crashes over me like the sound of glass shattering.

This was it. This was his escape plan.

And I don't want to escape. The certainty washes over me like a bucket of cold water. Every nerve ending on my skin screams in protest. *Wrong, wrong, wrong.* I don't know if we'll ever make it to freedom on this train. Don't know if I'll ever see the New York Public Library, but in this moment none of that matters.

Hades. He matters. And the pain he'll feel when I'm gone.

The pain I feel speeding away from him.

"Decker," I say carefully, wide awake, painfully awake. "I don't know if this is a good idea. He's going to catch up with this. And when he does—"

He stands up, the motion sudden enough to shock me. The backs of my knees hit one of the crates and I go down hard enough to wince. The wood is unforgiving. Then Decker is right there, throwing his arms around me. My body wants to relax into him, but I can't.

He waits until I can't resist him anymore.

"Don't think too much." He shakes his head against my neck, pressing a kiss there. "Don't worry. It's all going to work out in the end. You just have to trust me."

I don't have a choice.

There's no way out of a moving train, and no way away from Decker. No sudden moves. No sudden moves at all. I let him hold me, then sit next to me, and I try my best not to do anything at all. But with every moment that passes, I know one thing: I don't trust him. There's a desperation in his movements that make me nervous.

Time blurs, erasing the distinctions between moments. Still, I recognize the landscape around us. We get close to my mother's house, to the platform in the woods.

I hold my breath, waiting for the train to slow.

It doesn't slow. We speed past.

"Good fucking riddance to that place, too," Decker says under his breath.

What does that mean?

I press my lips together and clutch my stomach, trying not to be sick. It shouldn't feel this way, heading toward freedom. It shouldn't feel like I'm going in the wrong direction. Keeping it together becomes my first priority. Second priority; figure out a plan. Eventually, Decker is going to get off the train. Right? He has to. He's not going to ride it back to the mountain.

But I am.

A weight lifts off my shoulders the second the idea comes to me. I'll just stay on the train. I might get punished for it, but I'll get back to the mountain. I'll finish what I started.

My body aches from sitting by the time the train rolls into the city. It's been hours. My heart lifts despite my stiff legs and the pain in my back from sitting on the crate at an awkward angle. I've thought my new plan through from every angle. I will step off the train with him, and at the last moment I'll jump back on. He'll have no choice but to let me go. It'll be another long ride with the crates, and then I can go back to sleep. After Hades deals with me. A shiver of anticipation runs down my spine.

The train comes to a stop, and I pull the coat tighter around my body. The air is cool for the summer, and my outfit isn't exactly the one I'd choose to be running around the city in. Thank god I'll only spend a few moments on the platform.

Decker opens the door.

Get out, then get back in. I chant it to myself over and over.

He puts his hand on the small of my back and the look he gives me is so *off* it's all I can do not to flinch away. But I don't. I walk out with my head held high.

Onto a dark train platform.

That's not right.

At first it seems right, because so many of the places in the mountain were dark. Here, it's not right. There should be lights. Decker steps out in front of me and whistles, the sound like one of the birds in the forest by my mother's house.

"Deck, this seems weird." My voice only trembles a little. "I'm going to get back on the train."

He turns around, movements jerky, and clamps a hand around my wrist. "You're not."

I pull it back, fresh panic turning my stomach.

"Decker, let go." I try to yank my wrist out of his grip, but he's too strong. He doesn't look strong compared to Hades. But he doesn't need to be strong compared to Hades, does he? He only needs to be strong compared to me.

No. *No.*

The train whistle sounds and I move on instinct, rushing toward it. Decker doesn't quite know what to do with his arm and he loses his grip. I sprint for the door, picking up speed.

I make it two steps before my toe catches an uneven board on the platform.

My knees hit with a crack and the air goes out of me. I'm going to have to walk back. Back where? Back to my mother's house at least. Back to the mountain at worst. There's no way it'll be better climbing. But I can't stay here. I wait for Decker to lift me up, to dust me off, but he doesn't touch me.

He leaves me to get to my feet alone.

My knees are killing me.

"Deck?"

I turn around. Maybe he's gone. Maybe I can get back on the train.

Or maybe he's standing there with four other men, all of them looking at me.

"Decker." Horror closes my throat and brings tears to my eyes. I don't let them fall. "What did you do?"

I loved him. I *loved* him. Or maybe I never even knew him.

He shrugs, hands in his pockets. There's a new bulge there I didn't see before. Empty pockets, now full. He's a stranger to me.

"I had to get paid, Persephone. You have to understand that." Money—his pockets are full of money. Cash.

"Paid for what?" He looks down at the floor. "Paid for what, Decker?"

The train pulls away behind me.

The men with Decker step forward, advancing one by one.

And I have nowhere to go.

24

HADES

THE ONE NIGHT I want to lie down, some foreman in the mines can't handle himself.

I take my work seriously. Seriously enough that when the call came in, I left Persephone sleeping in her bed. I did not want to do that. Fuck no. If I took my work less seriously, I'd have told them to go fuck themselves while I woke her up for another round. I needed to keep my mind blank, and they stole that from me. My one concession was to leave Conor guarding her door.

It's not blank now.

I feel...alive. Awake. Obnoxiously so. All of my senses are turned up to maximum input. Every light is too bright, every sound too loud, and every distance is too great. I need her next to me.

And I've finally accepted it.

In reality, I was forced to accept it when fucking her took me over the edge into something like ecstasy. I haven't felt that in years. With any woman. It's like discovering a brand-new craving that's been there all along.

Like I've needed her all along, but now I'm finding her.

It doesn't make any fucking sense, and it doesn't need to. I'm going to fuck her until I figure out what to do about this little conundrum. Eventually, Demeter will have to know. She won't be thrilled. But I'll come up with a counteroffer. I'll buy her cooperation. I should have pushed harder on a deal already to avoid her temper tantrum. Live and learn.

Those jackasses down in the mines learned something tonight. They learned that if they fuck around enough, I'll come to set them straight. The ones that lived will pay far better attention to the foreman from now on.

I rub my eyes on the way back to my quarters. I want a shower. I want darkness. I need it. The house has been designed for me, and still, the lights become a problem. The special bulbs only delay the inevitable.

They switch off one by one as I approach, which is how I need things to be right now. Though I hate thinking in terms of *need*. I suppose it's something I'll have to get used to, now that I've gone ahead and fucked Persephone senseless. Can't give that up now.

I'm looking forward to being alone for the ten minutes it will take to get clean, then destroy her room a little more.

Only Oliver is waiting outside the double doors to my rooms. No sign of Conor.

"What is it?" His face is pale, almost green, the scar across his cheek standing out, angry and red. "Did those fuckers in the mines give you any more trouble?"

"One of them did," he says. "He's dead."

"Well, yes, Oliver. I thought you saw that I paid a visit."

"A different one. And one of the maids is missing, too. We have a situation on our hands."

"Which maid?" I don't give a fuck about the maids.

But I very much give a fuck when Oliver's gaze slips toward Persephone's bedroom.

"Her personal maid? What the fuck?"

I wrench her door open before I know what I'm doing. The frame shrieks in my hand. It's supposed to be strong enough to withstand anything, but it's not. Not today.

She's not here.

I tear the blankets off, the sheets, the pillows—they still smell like her. Like new leaves and sunshine and something unbearably sweet. I claw the fitted sheet off the bed and shove the mattress off the boxspring. She should be here. She should be here *somewhere.*

She's not here.

The closet comes apart under my hands. There hasn't been time for her to wear all the dresses that fall like feathers onto the carpet, but they all carry her scent. I yank every one of them off the hangers.

I search behind every cupboard. If she's here, anywhere, I don't care what I have to destroy to find her.

She's not here.

She's not here.

A cold dread, colder than the hand of death, grips the back of my neck.

Running footsteps announce Oliver. He looks worse than before, if it's possible. "I got a call." His face twists, and I don't know if it's fear or grief or both. "We have to—we have to go to the platform."

"Did our people find her?"

"No. They found—fuck, Luther." A rare slip, calling me that. "Conor."

I'm not aware of the mad rush to the platform, only the searing pain in my lungs. In my heart. Everywhere. A group of people are huddled around something on the ground. They're standing in a growing pool of blood.

Most of them try to get out of the way when they see me coming. The ones who don't, I throw to the side. One man goes over completely. I don't fucking care. The last one standing—kneeling, really—is the veterinarian I keep on the mountain. He owes me a great deal. I've never seen his face so bloodless until I'm gripping his white coat, pain's fists around my own neck. I could die of it.

"What happened?"

"Someone shot him." Three words, like rocks on glass. My head throbs, splintering. Too much light. I twist around without letting him go.

"Who was it?"

Oliver's right there, right behind us.

"The person who took her. The same person who took her." His voice shakes. He knows what this means.

I let go of Dr. Martin. Conor tried to stop them. No fucking doubt in my mind. I ignore the blood and stroke Conor's head anyway, numb horror seeping in at the edges of my consciousness. I can't tell if he's still alive. My own heartbeat is too fucking loud.

"They left on the train," says Oliver.

"Did you find her, then?" I'm numb. I'm on fire. I'm beneath the ground.

"No." To his credit, he moves where I can see him to deliver the final blow. He looks me in the eye. "She's gone."

THANK you so much for reading KING OF SHADOWS! The deliciously dangerous story of Hades & Persephone continues in SUMMER QUEEN, available now!

"Summer Queen is a sexy shot of anti-hero goodness—this is the kinky, delicious retelling of the year!" –Sierra Simone, USA Today bestselling author

Persephone's been stolen from me.

Out of my mountain, out of my reach. I'll do anything to get her back, even break a truce that's kept my kingdom safe.

I can only breathe again when she's back in my arms.

When I can make her pay for every second I spent in fear.

I want more than her body given to me in debt. I want her heart. And I will punish her until it's mine.

Order Summer Queen now!

For more books by Amelia Wilde,
visit her online at
www.awilderomance.com.

Printed in Poland
by Amazon Fulfillment
Poland Sp. z o.o., Wrocław